Wishes,
Kisses,
and Pigs

Betsy Hearne

Wishes, Kisses, and Pigs

Margaret K. McElderry Books
New York London Toronto Sydney Singapore

ALSO BY BETSY HEARNE
ELIZA'S DOG
LISTENING FOR LEROY
(MARGARET K. MCELDERRY BOOKS)

Margaret K. McElderry Books
An imprint of Simon & Schuster Children's Publishing Division
1230 Avenue of the Americas, New York, New York 10020

Book design by Michael Nelson
The text for this book is set in Perpetua.

Printed in the United States of America
10 9 8 7 6 5 4 3 2 1

Library of Congress Cataloging-in-Publication Data
Hearne, Betsy Gould.
Wishes, kisses, and pigs / by Betsy Hearne
p. cm.
Summary: After eleven-year-old Louise makes a wish on the first
evening star and her brother turns into a pig, she uses wishes, kisses,
and spells to try to put things right again.
ISBN 0-689-84122-1
[1. Wishes—Fiction. 2. Magic—Fiction. 3. Brothers and sisters—Fiction.
4. Pigs—Fiction.] I. Title.
PZ7.H3464 Wi 2001
[Fic]—dc21
00-032460

For my grandchildren, and theirs

CONTENTS

Wishes,
Kisses,
and Pigs

CHAPTER 1

The Star

"I know what you're doing," said Willie.

"No, you don't," said Louise.

"Yes, I do. You're wishing on a star."

"No, I'm not. The sun's just going down—look, it's red as fire."

"Red as a rotten tomato," said Willie. "SPLAT goes the tomato. SQUOOSH, the sky's all mushy." Willie pulled one of his sister's pigtails.

"Stop it, Willie."

"SPLISH, here comes the first star," said Willie. "PLOP, here comes Louise. Oh, please, says Louise, I wish for a kiss." Willie pulled Louise's other pigtail, and she jerked away.

"I do not, Willie, that's disgusting. And you don't even know how to make a wish, anyway."

"Neither do you."

"Yes, I do," said Louise. "Star light, star bright, first star I've seen tonight. I wish I may, I wish I might, have the wish I wish tonight."

Willie's blond hair glowed white in the evening light. He was chewing on a sassafras twig. Willie was a hefty boy, always chewing on something. "Sunsets are boring," he said, "and so are you. I'm going to feed the pigs." He turned his back on her and walked away.

Louise felt a dark rage rising. "You ARE a pig."

Her voice had surprising power, but Willie didn't answer. He had already disappeared in the trees. The wind blew. The leaves whispered. The owl that haunted their hills called *whoo*.

Louise Tolliver watched the sky. Behind her loomed Old Giant, the mountain that shadowed their little house, barn, and garden. Tollivers' Hollow was said to be a peculiar place, even a perilous place, but it didn't feel peculiar or perilous to her. It felt like home. Between the last pink light and the blue night shone the moon, curving thin and white as the end of a fingernail. A new June moon. And sure enough, below it was the evening star, looking like a diamond ring on somebody's finger. Why not? thought Louise. Star light, star bright, first star I've seen tonight, I wish I may, I wish I might, have the wish I wish tonight.

"Beware of what you've wished for," glittered the star.

"I haven't wished for anything yet," said Louise.

The star was silent.

"Oh, well," said Louise. "Willie's right. It's silly to wish on a star, anyway."

CHAPTER 2

Missing Willie

Louise finished the milking and leaned her head into the honey-colored hollow of Molly Cow's warm flank. Cows were so much better than brothers. There was nothing more comforting than a sweet cow, especially a cow named Molly. Molly was old now, but before her, there had been another Molly. There had been generations of cows named Molly in the Tolliver family, as long as anybody could remember. And always a boy named Jack. Daddy's name was Jack, and Louise was sure that Mama and Daddy had planned to have another Jack someday. But that was before Daddy disappeared seven years ago.

She stood up and moved around to face Molly, who watched her with deep dark eyes. Surely this

Molly had the longest eyelashes ever, even if her back was bony and her joints were stiff. Louise could remember being small enough to ride on Molly's back and walk under her stomach, but not anymore. Louise kept growing, and Molly was a small cow, small and shapely. She had horns that curved out and in like a harp. They were sharp, but Molly Cow was so gentle that no one ever thought to cut them off. She never needed a cowbell because she came when they called. Sometimes she even lowed in the field to let them know where she was. Molly had a long, soft moo like a lullaby.

Louise picked up the milk bucket. She carried it carefully along the pathway and through the back door, where Mama waited in the kitchen.

"Have you seen Willie?" asked Mama. "That boy can disappear quicker than greased lightning."

"He was up on the hill being his mean old self about an hour ago," said Louise. "Then he went off to feed the pigs."

"Well, it's not like him to skip supper. He's usually sitting at the table with a knife and fork in his hand before I even finish cooking."

"Let's just eat, Mama. He'll come home when he's hungry." Louise sat down and took a long drink of buttermilk. It was nice not to have a brother around bothering her at the dinner table. The corn bread tasted sweeter, the sweet potatoes tasted creamier, the ham tasted spicier, the green beans . . . well, the green beans tasted like green beans, but you can't have everything.

After they finished, Louise did the dishes and Mama went out to call Willie. Louise could hear his name echo back from the hills all around the hollow where they lived. "Willie, Willie, Willie, WillieWillieWillie!" Then the hills were silent, because no one answered back. Only the owl, which they heard but never saw, hooted somewhere in the treetops. Louise was used to the sound, but still it seemed eerie to hear it call all evening. Something had disturbed it.

Mama came in looking worried. "It's dark now, Louise. I can't see a thing. I just don't know what to do. He can't be lost. Willie knows those woods like the back of his hand. He's been hunting out there since he was knee-high to a grasshopper."

"Don't worry, Mama. Suppose he trailed a possum or something that took him up Old Giant. He'd just camp out and come home tomorrow morning."

Mama looked out the window. The top ridge of the mountain was barely visible, stretched out above them like a stone giant fallen down to Earth. "You don't reckon he fell off a cliff somewhere?"

"You know he'd just bounce, Mama."

"I mean it, Louise. I'm going down the mountain to call Sheriff Tod Watkins if Willie doesn't show up soon."

"That sheriff couldn't find a needle in a haystack, Mama. Willie will show up. You just wait and see."

CHAPTER 3

Visitors

Willie didn't show up. Come morning, Sheriff Tod Watkins did, though, in his old red truck. "Howdy, Clara, always a pleasure to see you—looking pretty as ever. And Louise, you're looking . . . you're looking more like your . . . uh . . . daddy . . . every day."

"Thank you, Tod, we take that as a compliment," Mama said stiffly. "Jack Tolliver was, and probably still is, a very good-looking man."

"Well, Clara, beauty is in the eye of the beholder, as we all know."

"We all know less than we think we do, Tod."

"Now, you know I'd rather be friendly than fuss with you. It was your call that brought me out here, after all, though I'd come a lot more often if you'd let me."

"I called you in your capacity as sheriff, Tod, and like I told you on the phone, I'm worried stiff about Willie. He didn't come home all night, and we can't find hide nor hair of him."

"Seems like there's always somebody disappearing from this hollow."

"We're talking about my boy Willie."

"Yes, but boys will be boys. When did you see him last?"

"Louise talked to him about sundown yesterday, then he went off to feed the pigs."

"We'd better have a look around, then." The sheriff made a beeline for the barn, with Mama and Louise following along behind him in the hot sun. The barn was quiet but for some flies buzzing around and Molly Cow switching them off with her tail. Louise threw her arm around Molly's neck and scratched between her harp horns. It was past time to turn Molly out to pasture. The sheriff climbed up the wooden ladder to the hayloft and spent some time poking around. Then he came back down and scratched his head. "There's no boys up there," he said.

"We know that, Tod, we looked there first," said Mama, "thinking maybe he'd fallen asleep."

Louise looked at the sheriff scratching his head. Then she looked at Mama with "I told you so" written all over her eyes. Mama sighed.

"Let's snoop around the pigpen, then, and see what there is to see," said the sheriff.

The pigpen was knee-deep in mud from all the rain lately. A brown sow lay on her side with eleven newborn shoats sucking and squealing and pushing and shoving. The sow snorted and rolled herself up when she saw Mama and Louise coming. She poked her nose through the fence, looking for food, while the little shoats tumbled around her.

Suddenly out of the trees charged a big white pig, straight toward them.

"Whoa!" shouted the sheriff. "Looks like one of your pigs got loose, Clara."

The pig stopped dead in its tracks and stared up at Louise, pushing at her leg with its round, pink snout.

"That's not our pig, Tod," said Mama. "Must be one of the neighbors got a new one that wandered off."

"I'll ask around," said the sheriff. "We better pen it up so it doesn't run loose in the woods. I don't see any tracks, except pig tracks. No boy tracks. Naturally, there'd be pig tracks with a pig running around here."

Louise rolled her eyes at Mama.

"How do you propose to go about finding Willie?" asked Mama.

"I'll tell you what, Clara, the first thing is to go talk to all the neighbors and see if maybe he's gone visiting and forgot to let you know. He didn't talk about running away or anything, did he?"

"First of all, Willie wouldn't go off visiting without telling me about it," said Mama, "and secondly, he wouldn't run away because he's the man in this family and he knows we'd have a hard time without him."

"But Willie does have a girlfriend."

"You know he's been sweet on your niece Maybelle Watkins since she was born, practically, but I don't see what that has to do with it."

Louise made a little gagging sound just thinking about Maybelle Watkins's round, pink face.

Mama glared at her and then at the sheriff. "He's a good boy, Tod, you know that as well as I do."

"Now, Clara, don't get your feathers ruffled up. I'm just thinking through the possibilities here. If you don't mind I'll check with my brother Tom on the whereabouts of his little Miss Maybelle. We've got to start somewhere, the sooner the better." The sheriff marched toward his old red truck like Mama was wasting his precious time and started the engine with a roar. "I'll be back soon as I find out something," he called out the window, and then he took off down the road with mud splurting around the wheels.

"That'll be never," said Louise.

"All we can do is hope for the best, though I'd like

to hope for someone better than Tod Watkins to track down Willie," said Mama. "Look, here comes that pig again. We better get him penned up. Run fetch the slop bucket and pour some buttermilk over yesterday's corn bread. That'll lure him through the gate."

The pig trotted around and around Mama, then followed her obediently back to the pen. When Louise brought the slop bucket, Mama was scratching his back.

"I declare, Louise, this is the cleanest pig I ever saw. And the friendliest. He just sits here right beside me. We might not even need the slop bucket."

But they did. When Mama opened the gate and tried to walk the pig in, he backed up. He ran around the fence outside the pen in a worried way, but never took off into the woods. Instead, he kept coming back to Louise and Mama, nudging first one and then the other with his snout.

"Try the slop trick, then," said Mama.

Louise held out the bucket. The pig stuck his head in right off and started going after the soupy corn bread like nobody's business. Louise backed through the gate. The pig came after her with his head in the bucket, smacking and chewing and swallowing as fast as he could. Slam! Mama closed the gate, and Louise climbed over the fence clanking the empty bucket.

The pig looked at Louise through the fence slats with sad little pig eyes.

"This pig has sky-blue eyes, Mama. I never saw a pig with sky-blue eyes before."

"Me, neither, honey, but there's lots of things I never saw. Come on in before you get sunstroke out here. Let's see if we can figure out where your brother might have gone."

The old sow snuffled the new pig in a friendly way, and the little shoats piled around him, but the new pig paid no attention. He just rested his snout on the fence slat and gazed mournfully up at the house.

CHAPTER 4

Suspicions

Mama and Louise pushed the porch swing back and forth with their feet. The crickets sang, and the swing squeaked in a peaceful way, but there was worry in the evening air.

"Did Willie say anything to you before he went off to feed the pigs?" asked Mama.

"Not a word."

"He must have said something. What were you two talking about?"

"Nothing, just a stupid old argument."

"What kind of argument?"

"He was teasing me about wishing on a star, and I told him to go away so I could watch the sunset in peace."

"Then what?"

"That's all. Then he left."

"Was he mad?"

"No, *I* was mad. It was his fault for coming around bothering me. He said sunsets were boring and I was boring and he was going to feed the pigs, and I said he was . . . ," Louise trailed off.

"What?"

" . . . a pig."

Mama and Louise looked at each other.

"I didn't really wish it."

"Maybe you just kind of decreed it and that star happened to be listening."

"It couldn't be," said Louise.

"Anything's possible. I surely never saw a sky-eyed pig before."

"A pig with sky-blue eyes, you mean?"

"That's what I mean," said Mama.

"Like Willie's?"

"Like Willie's."

Louise sat still and wondered. The porch swing squeaked because Mama kept pushing it. The owl *whoo'd,* and Molly Cow answered from the barn with a long, low moo.

"Mama, what if Willie really did turn pig? What makes a wish come true? How come some wishes come true and some don't and you never know which one is going to do which?"

"I can't answer that, Louise. It's a fancy question, and I'm a plain person."

"Mama, you're beautiful! Everybody says so."

"That's neither here nor there. I have a plain heart and I do what it tells me to. Your daddy, now, he could have sorted this out."

"If only he were here."

"Don't I wish that every day of my life."

"What are we going to do about Willie?"

"We'll study the situation," said Mama. "If what you think might someway be true *is* true, at least he's safe and sound and not hanging off a cliff somewhere."

"And he's not hungry," said Louise. "That counts for a lot with Willie."

CHAPTER 5

The New Pig

Before Louise finished emptying the slop bucket into the pig trough, the old sow and the new pig had their snouts down in the sour milk and apple peels and eggshells and moldy cheese and stale bread and wilted greens and burnt piecrusts and other items of interest.

"Willie?" said Louise. "Are you Willie? Give me a sign."

The pig looked up at her but kept eating. He was no longer clean. Mud stuck to his belly, and gobs of slop dropped from his jaws.

"I swear, Willie—if you are Willie—you like that slop just as much as you liked Mama's good meals at the table," said Louise. "And stop drooling."

The pig grunted happily and licked the sides of the

feed trough. Then he moved toward the gate and butted his head against it.

"No, I can't let you out. No telling what you'd do. If you ran away Mama would have my hide, and also—if you are Willie—I wouldn't have a brother anymore at all. It'd be bad enough having a brother that not only acts like a pig but looks like one, too."

The pig rubbed his chin thoughtfully on the fence slats. Louise patted his head.

"Those ears of yours sure feel soft," said Louise. "They say you can't make a silk purse out of a sow's ear, but yours might make a nice purse." The pig backed away to the other side of the pen.

"Don't worry, I'm not going to cut off your ears."

The pig turned his back on her.

"And don't get into a sulk, either. Mama and I are thinking about what to do. We don't know whether you really are Willie or not, anyway. If only you could talk!"

The pig turned back around.

He stared up at the sky.

His brow furrowed.

His throat clenched up, and he made a little strangling sound.

Louise watched him closely.

The strangling sound turned to a gargle, then a gasp and some heavy panting.

"Uhnk, uhnk, uhnk," said the pig.

"What?" asked Louise.

"Unh, unh."

"Unh, unh, yourself," said Louise.

"Um Woolly."

"You're not woolly. You've hardly got a hair on your hide."

"AM WELLY!"

"I'm . . . Willie?"

"Uss."

"Yes? Willy? Is it really you? Are you saying something? Or am I just making this up? I can hardly figure out what you're saying. If it's you, Willie, you have to try harder. You know, you don't look too much like your old self except for a big stomach and those sky-blue eyes."

The pig worked his mouth around and wrinkled up his snout. "Hud wuk," he huffed.

"Sure, it's hard work, Willie, you never were too good at talking, anyway. You have to practice. It's probably like learning one of those foreign languages. Latin or French or Italian or something. In school you even had trouble with English."

The pig glared at her.

"Don't get huffy. You know that's true. If it hadn't been for Maybelle Watkins you'd have failed English."

"Maybelle," the pig said clearly.

"Honestly, Willie, I don't see how you can stand that girl. She's so hoity-toity, it's hard to bear. And greedy. Come to think of it, she looks a little bit like a pig. Except for those floppy curls—I bet they're real soft, too, like your ears."

The pig took on a dreamy look and nodded his head.

"Yuk," said Louise.

"Yum," said the pig.

"You deserve to be a pig, Willie—it's fitting you should have a piggy girlfriend. If we ever get you out of this fix, it won't change a thing on the inside, just the outside is all."

The pig grunted.

"You better stop that grunting and work on your English. I'm going up to the house and tell Mama what I've found out. She'll be relieved, I guess, even though she kind of knew already. They say a mama knows her child anywhere, and you weren't too hard to fathom."

Louise picked up the slop bucket and turned to go. Willie wandered toward the pig trough to see if there were any little morsels of food left. The old sow and her shoats were sound asleep. Willie lay down in the warm mud, snuggling deeper till he made a comfy wallow. Pretty soon he closed his little sky-blue eyes with their little white eyelashes. The sun beamed down, the birds tittered. Willie had hardly ever felt so peaceful in all his hardworking life. More slops would be good. The only thing he really missed was Maybelle. Mama was right nearby. Louise was herself, bossier than usual but bearable so long as she remembered to feed him. But he was lonely for Maybelle.

CHAPTER 6

Fooling Folks

"Hey, Mama, you don't have to worry about Willie anymore!" Louise was breathing hard from running into the house.

"What do you mean?"

"It's like I thought. He just turned pig, is all. He's all right otherwise. He can even say a few words and he's trying to talk better."

Mama closed her eyes. "Bless his heart. I was so fearful he'd gone off and gotten hurt. We have to figure out what to do about him now, and we better not tell anybody. They'd think we were crazy. Or else those city reporters would come out here taking pictures and making a fuss and we'd never have a minute's peace of mind. There'd probably be all kinds of scientists from the university poking at poor Willie's insides."

"That would be a treat," said Louise.

"Now, Louise, you have to be kind. You got him into this mess to begin with."

"I know it, Mama, and I feel bad. I've been thinking maybe I should try the same thing again—you know, wish on the star but this time be real clear about what it is I want."

"It wouldn't hurt to try. Like I said, I'm just too plain-minded to know how these things work."

At that moment they heard a grinding of shifted gears, a churning of wheels, and a roaring engine that suddenly went dead. Everything was quiet again except for a pinecone that fell on the tin roof, thunk, then a knock at the door, thunk, thunk.

"That'll be Tod," said Mama, "come back to report on nothing. We have to be real careful now, Louise."

"He won't suspect a thing, Mama. He never does—even though that's his job."

Mama went to open the door. "Come in, Tod, we've been waiting to hear something. We've been real anxious about Willie. Did you find anything out?"

The sheriff stepped into the living room and studied his muddy shoes for some time.

"Tod?" said Mama.

"I hate to tell you this, Clara, but nobody knows a

thing. Nobody's seen him or heard from him. I talked to all the neighbors. I talked to my brother, Tom, and he swears his little Maybelle has been tucked away home for the duration. I guess we're going to have to call in the Feds if you think this could be a case of kidnapping."

"I don't know how anybody could drag that boy anywhere he didn't want to go," said Mama.

"Or why anybody would want to," said Louise.

"We don't have a cent to our names," said Mama, "so there would be no point."

"I know that, Clara, that's why I asked you right off whether he might've left of his own accord, so to speak. Not to be disrespectful."

Mama went quiet and appeared to be deep in thought.

Louise stared at her feet. She could feel a little smile coming on. She tried to think about something sad. All she could think of was her brother's snout in the pig trough. That didn't help at all. Fortunately, Mama started talking again.

"You know, Tod, I've been thinking about what you said."

"About what?"

"About Willie, of course. That's who we're talking about, isn't it?"

"Yes, Clara, I see what you mean. I just had to make sure. That's my business, to make sure."

The little smile inside Louise turned to a smirk. She pulled down the corners of her mouth.

"I know how upsetting this must be for you and the little lady here," the sheriff said, looking at Louise.

"We're feeling it pretty hard," said Mama. "But since it looks like he left of his own accord, we shouldn't bother you about it anymore, Tod. We surely wouldn't want to drag in somebody from outside, the Feds or whoever. You're best for the job, and if you're sure there's no foul play . . ."

"I could swear to it, Clara. That boy is big enough to take care of himself, or anybody else who tried to tackle him. And like you said, there's no reason . . . with all due respect."

"That's a big relief to my mind," Mama said earnestly. "I'm sure you're right, now that I study it some. He might even have figured on fooling the army, and tried to join up just to bring us in a little cash. He wouldn't have told me, of course, since I'd never let him go. Soon as they figure out his real age, he'll be back on this doorstep again."

"There you are, Clara. I knew you'd see it that way. Just let me know when he comes home, hear? We'll all be waiting."

The sheriff scuffed his feet on the welcome mat on his way back out, having forgotten to do it on the way in. Then, just as Mama had almost closed the door and Louise's smile was about to cut loose, he turned back around. "What about that pig, Clara?"

Mama's face went cold. "What about that pig, Tod?"

"None of the neighbors seemed to know anything about the pig, either. My brother, Tom, did remember he'd lost a pig some time ago."

"How long ago?" asked Mama

"Quite a while back, he wasn't exactly sure."

"This looks like a new pig to me, I mean a young pig."

"Big, though, you have to admit, a big pig. Anyway, Tom may come over one of these days and take a look."

"Well, don't worry, we'll take good care of him," said Mama.

"I hate to think of you having another mouth to fill," said the sheriff. "I could make a pen down by the jail and feed him out of county funds. You know there's always the Labor Day picnic to plan for. We could have us a town barbecue."

Mama turned pale. Her hands clenched into fists, one on each side. Her chin came up, and her eyes went sharp. "No, thank you, Tod. Finders keepers, as you well know."

"Seems like the pig found you, Clara, so I guess you belong to the pig, no offense."

"None taken."

"Just trying to do right by you, ma'am. But I guess if you feed the pig, time will come that the pig feeds you. Ha-ha."

"Good-bye, Tod, you've been a big help," Mama said. She closed the door and leaned against it while they both listened to the truck engine roar away down the muddy road.

CHAPTER 7

Waiting

Louise walked through the wet woods toward the hill. Evening after evening she waited for the first star so she could make another wish. Evening after evening the clouds rolled over the sky as if rain would never stop falling. The sun seemed to have set forever. The owl had fallen silent. One dark evening, after waiting in vain to glimpse a star in the black sky, Louise took a different way home. Halfway there, she caught her foot in a tangle of bushes and fell flat on her face.

"Doggone it! We could use a little moonlight around here." She tugged her foot loose, and something came with it. The strap on a pair of overalls.

"Oh, lordy," said Louise, "I wondered what happened to Willie's clothes." She felt around in the bushes and found a raggedy shirt and a pair of under-pants burst open at the waistband.

"He must have run around in the woods with his clothes half on and half off—and half scared out of his wits, too. Poor Willie." She rolled the clothes into a wet ball and tucked them under her arm. On her way past the pigpen she stopped and held them up to show Willie. "Look what I found, big brother."

The pig hung his head.

"Come on, now, Willie, we'll just clean these up and you'll fit back into them one of these days. Mama and I made a plan. It just takes time to work these things out."

Willie heaved a big pig sigh.

"For Pete's sake, say something, Willie! You haven't been practicing at all, have you? You're going to forget how to talk pretty soon if you don't try harder."

Willie rolled his mouth around and appeared to be chewing on his tongue. "Only," he said finally.

"Only what?"

Willie shook his head. "L-lonely."

"Poor Willie. You've got to think on the bright side. What about the old sow? She's some kind of company, and the shoats are cute."

Willie looked at her.

"And there's Mama sometimes, and me. Of course

we can't sit out here with you all the time, but there's Molly Cow. Molly Cow likes grazing over there by the trees."

Willie glanced over at Molly Cow and shook his head.

"I tell you what, Willie. How about if I bring you a nice bucket of slop and we can have a little chat."

Louise dashed into the house, dumped the clothes bundle on the kitchen table, grabbed the bucket from its place beside the stove, and ran back out again with the slops sloshing over the rim. Willie's face brightened when he saw the bucket, and he moved automatically toward the feeding trough. So did the old sow and all the little shoats with her.

Louise held out the bucket, but she didn't pour the slops. "Not till you talk to me, Willie."

Willie's round body stiffened, and his little sky-blue eyes turned red. The old sow began to tremble, squealing for food.

"Mean!" Willie said after a moment of loud sound filled the farm air.

"It's for your own good," said Louise. "You have to keep talking, Willie. You'll turn into a real pig if you don't watch out."

Willie charged toward Louise and crashed into the fence slats.

"Stop it, Willie! I'm sorry. I didn't mean to say

that. You're not really a pig. I mean, you are now but you weren't when I said you were before you got to be one. Here, let me rub your head. You banged it so hard, you almost knocked yourself out."

Willie drooped. Louise poured slop into the trough, and the sow buried her snout in it, but Willie did not. He let Louise rub his head and soft ears, then wandered over to the mud puddle in the middle of the pen and lay down in it.

Louise picked up the empty bucket and walked slowly toward the house. When she opened the kitchen door, she saw her mother sitting at the table, looking down at the bundle of dirty old wet clothes.

CHAPTER 8

Wrong Again

"There's bound to be a break in the weather soon," said Louise.

And there was. The sun sang up one morning, and Mama sang while she worked in the garden and Louise sang to Willie in the pigpen.

"Tonight's the night, Willie, I'm sure of it. I know we can fix this situation if I just undo the wish, or re-wish, or whatever. I'll be sitting up there on that hill this evening waiting out the sunset for that first star, and you'll be human quick as a wink. Come to think of it, I better hang those clothes over the fence so you're not standing there stark naked by the time I get back. Mama washed them, and they'll get dry as a bone in this sunshine."

Louise swirled through her chores. She cleaned out Molly Cow's stall and put fresh straw down. She even helped Mama with the weeding, just to pass the time. The heat seeped through her hair till she had to put a hat on, which she hated. The hat had two ear holes and two horn holes that she had once cut for Molly Cow to wear on hot days. It looked a lot better on Molly Cow, to tell the truth, but fashion was the least of Louise's concerns. Making the evening come quicker was the main thing. She even cleaned the house while Mama spent time in the kitchen making every one of Willie's favorite dishes. His favorite human dishes. Fried okra, fried green tomatoes, fried potatoes, fry bread, and fried pies. Also fried bacon.

"I'm not so sure about the bacon anymore, Mama," said Louise.

"I see your point, Louise. That's mighty thoughtful of you. We'll just switch the menu here a little bit till we see what's what. I'm going to make my Blue-Ribbon Chocolate Cake for sure, though."

"Yum," said Louise. "Nobody can beat that cake."

"But you have to beat the batter," said Mama.

"And count your blessings while you're beating the batter!" said Louise.

"You remembered the recipe." Mama beamed.

"I will never forget it," said Louise. She remembered every word. On Fair Day, when the judge awarded Mama the blue ribbon and asked how she made that wonderful chocolate cake, Mama said, "It's not a secret, but it's hard to explain. It's butter and sugar and eggs and chocolate and vanilla and flour and soda and salt and milk, but it's more than that, too. You take what you have and what you know and what you feel and what you guess and you mix them all together, and remember to look out the window and listen to the birds sing while you're doing it. Plus, it doesn't hurt to count your blessings while you're beating the batter."

Mama started gathering the ingredients while Louise went to put Molly Cow in the barn. It was not time for milking yet, but Louise had to do something. She was too fidgety to stay in one place for long. Molly Cow didn't seem to mind. She lay down peacefully on the clean straw in the big wooden stall and chewed her cud.

The day slowly drained away. Long before the sun started down, Louise was swatting flies on the hill, waiting for the magic moment.

"Seems like you've taken a slowdown pill," she said to the sun. Little by little it began to glide lower in the sky. A few clouds gathered, but not rain clouds.

They were the little puffy kind that makes the reddest sunsets, red as fire—or maybe red as ripe tomatoes. One way or another, they surely did get red. Old Giant loomed above her, throwing shadows over hills and hollow, waiting for the sun to slide down its back out of sight.

Whoo-whoo, called the owl, so close that it seemed right beside her. Louise's heart skipped like a stone across the creek.

"Hush up!" she shouted at the owl. "Or else come on out here where I can see you."

The owl was silent. The sun was gone. Louise held her breath and raised her eyes to the darkening sky above.

"Come on, come on," she breathed. At long last she saw the moon, a new July moon, and then— PING—the first star. Louise suddenly felt nervous and tongue-tied, just like she had when she almost choked to death on her lines in the school play, right in front of everybody's parents. She took a deep breath and said the words so fast, they got jumbled up. "Star bright star light first star I've seen tonight I wish I may I wish I might have the wish I wish tonight.

"Wait, now, I'm not sure I got that right. Star LIGHT star BRIGHT first star in sight tonight I wish I may I wish I might have the wish I wish tonight.

"Oh, that's not right, either. Let me start all over again. Star LIGHT, star BRIGHT, first star I'VE SEEN tonight. I wish I may, I wish I might, have the wish I wish tonight. Okay, that's it. Please make that big fat muddy pig down in the pigpen in our hollow turn human. There now." Louise stood up and ran down the hill toward the pigpen as fast as she could.

Beside the pigpen stood a tubby old woman with hardly any hair and no clothes on at all. Mama was racing toward her with a blanket. The woman was looking around with dazed, squinty eyes.

"Oh, dear," said Louise.

"Oh, dear, is right," said Mama.

"Unh, unh, unh, unh," said the old woman.

All the little shoats were lined up in a row inside the fence, fussing and squealing, but the old sow was nowhere in sight. Just Willie, who had buried his snout in the mud and would not look up at all.

CHAPTER 9

Delilah

Mama and Louise sat at the table with their eyes drooping almost shut. They had been feeding baby pigs with an old baby bottle day and night. As soon as one got full, the others set up a piercing screech to be fed some more.

"Don't you reckon these shoats ever get tired of eating?" asked Louise.

"Seems not," said Mama. "Come to think of it, every time I ever looked out in that pen, either they were suckling her or she was sucking up slop just as fast as she could." Mama nodded her head toward the old woman, who was sound asleep on the floor. She had refused to sit in the rocker, climb into the bed, or come to the table. They had had a hard time getting her to leave the shoats and come inside. Every time she woke up, she sneaked out the back door and went to lie down as close to the fence as she could get. If they locked the door, she plunged her head into the slop bucket for whatever little tidbits had accumulated. Then she banged the bucket around in the kitchen and made a fearful racket. She didn't fit into any of Mama's clothes, so they had to pin the blanket on her like a dress, which she kept trying to take off.

"Seeing that she can't nurse the shoats anymore, maybe she could learn how to feed them with the baby bottle," said Louise.

"She doesn't use her hands real well," said Mama.

"What are we going to call her? We can't just say su-eee, su-eee anymore."

"She never did have a name, to tell the truth. We always just called her the old sow."

"That doesn't sound too polite now that she's human, Mama."

"So true, Louise."

"We should call her something real nice, so she'll get used to being human."

Mama considered. "How about Delilah? That always reminded me of the word "delightful." I was going to name you Delilah, but your daddy liked Louise."

Thank goodness, thought Louise, Daddy did something useful before he took off for parts unknown. "All right," she said after a little while, "Delilah will do. But what are we going to do about Willie?"

"I don't rightly know," said Mama. "You could try the star again and be a little more clear—name names and so on."

"That star is out to get me, Mama, honestly!"

"It sure seems vengeful. Or at least irritated."

"Also, what if I only get three wishes? The next one would be the last one, but now we've got two changes to make instead of one—this old woman is never going to be a happy human."

"I guess not. You can't teach an old dog new tricks," said Mama.

"Or pig, either," said Louise. "Anyway, I was thinking about all those stories where the person just has three chances and then the game is up. It seems like whatever I do now turns out wrong. Maybe we should save that last chance till we have it real clear in our minds what's the best thing to do—if there is a last chance."

"Well, I had an idea along those lines myself, of trying something else first. You know that fairy tale where the beauty kisses the beast and he changes back into a prince?"

"Yuk! Willie's my brother, and I'm not going to kiss his disgusting snout."

"I know that, but maybe we could get Maybelle to do it. She's his real truelove."

"Maybelle wouldn't get near a pig. She thinks she's the queen of the world, la-de-da." Louise pictured Maybelle prancing around the playground at school, calling Louise a baby. Just because Louise wasn't interested in dressing up and kissing boys—ugh, Louise would rather kiss Molly Cow! If that made her a baby, so be it. And what was there to dress up for in Tollivers' Hollow, anyway? Feeding the pigs? All that growing-up stuff could just wait a hundred years— especially if it meant kissing boys.

"You know, Louise," sighed Mama, "we might just have to trust Maybelle—tell her the truth and see if she can help us out here."

"Trust Maybelle? Maybelle *Watkins?*"

"Honey, sometimes you don't have a choice, and that includes in-laws, too, just in case Maybelle ever does help bring our Willie back . . . and gets to be your sister-in-law."

"Oh, no, Mama, how could you?"

"It's not me, it's Willie. If he sees something in Maybelle Watkins, we're bound to look for it, too."

"We'd have to use one of those magnifying glasses

from Miss Smith's science class. Or maybe borrow Doc Brady's microscope."

"We have to try nonetheless. We have to get Willie back and we might have to get Maybelle to help us."

"Well, even if she does, that's only one thing done," said Louise.

A snuffling, snorting snore arose from the floor.

"We've still got Delilah. And while we're at it," she continued, "there's another little problem. Willie's off his feed. He's pining away. His haunches are getting skinny, and his skin's starting to sag. Plus, his tail doesn't curl. It hangs straight down like limp string."

"That's a depressed pig," said Mama.

"He won't practice talking and he gets gloomier and gloomier every single minute."

"I'm feeling kind of puny about all this myself," said Mama, "but we just have to keep—"

Squeals of hunger interrupted her from the pig-pen.

" . . . feeding the baby pigs," said Louise. The figure on the floor was gathering herself for a mad dash to the pigpen.

CHAPTER 10

More Visitors

When Tom Watkins's old yellow truck drove up, Louise and Mama had just finished feeding all the shoats again, and Willie was staring at his reflection in a mud puddle. Mama grabbed Louise's hand and ran toward the house.

"See if you can get Delilah into my bedroom and lock the door, Louise, quick. Do the slop bucket trick while I stall Tom."

Louise scooped up the bucket on her way through the kitchen and raced toward Mama's bedroom. The old woman stuck her head inside and followed Louise right through Mama's bedroom door. Louise slammed it shut and locked it. She could hear Mama, who had gotten to the porch and closed the front door.

"Tom Watkins, we haven't seen you in a coon's

age, or Maybelle, either, since school let out. What brings you-all here?"

"We just came by to pay a friendly little visit, Clara. You know I'd come more often if you'd let me. A poor widower gets pretty lonesome with his two children growing up so fast. And Maybelle here has been dying to play with Louise."

Maybelle wrinkled up her nose as if she smelled something bad.

"What a coincidence," said Mama. "Louise has been wanting to talk to Maybelle, too. Louise?" she called. "Louise? Where can that girl have gone? She was here just a minute ago."

Louise came around the side of the house, jumped up on the porch, and stepped up beside Mama. She seemed a little out of breath.

"Haven't you been wanting to talk to Maybelle, Louise?"

Louise wrinkled up her nose as if she smelled the same thing Maybelle did. Mama put her arm around Louise to give her a little behave-yourself squeeze. Tom and Maybelle stared at Mama's hand, which still gripped the sticky baby bottle.

"Oh!" said Mama. She looked a little surprised herself. "I guess I forgot to put this in the kitchen. We were just . . . we were just . . ."

"Playing dolls," said Louise.

"Right, playing dolls," said Mama. "Nothing like using a real bottle, is there, Maybelle?"

"I wouldn't know, Mrs. Tolliver, I haven't played dolls for a long time," said Maybelle.

"Well, I'm sure you two young ladies can find something to do, Maybelle," said Tom. "Why don't you and Louise run on while Clara and I have us a little chat."

"Um, sure, Maybelle, why don't we go on out by the pigpen," said Louise.

"The pigpen! Don't you have a room with a chair in it where I could sit down?"

"I guess you can come on into my room."

"I guess I can," Maybelle said, and she stalked after Louise with her head held high.

Tom watched her go with pride in his eyes. Mama watched Tom, the spitting image of his twin brother, Tod.

"Well now, Clara," Tom said, turning to Mama. "How are things going without that big boy of yours? We were mighty sorry to hear that he took off and left without a word. I can tell you right now, no boy of mine would do that."

"Your boy, Luke, has cut a few capers in his time, Tom."

"Well, losing the man of the house must have set you back some. Losing my wife sure was a blow. Say, I bet you could use some help around here, and I've got two strong arms."

"You keep your arms to yourself, Tom. Louise and I manage well enough. And we haven't lost Willie. He's just temporarily misplaced."

"Seems like that's a problem that runs in the family. But speaking of losing, Clara, I seem to have lost a pig—maybe temporarily misplaced, you might say. Could we just step around back and see the pig that happened by your place recently?"

Without waiting to hear a reply, Tom stepped off the porch and headed toward the pigpen like a runaway tractor, with Mama trotting after him to keep up. The shoats were already getting hungry, and Willie was still gazing downcast at his reflection in the puddle. He hardly glanced up at the two humans leaning over the fence.

"Say, where's that old sow of yours?" Tom asked, glancing at the restless little shoats.

"She sort of comes and goes," said Mama. "Right now she's gone."

"I see that," said Tom. "Seems like there's a lot of pigs coming and going around here."

"Tod did mention you lost a pig," said Mama. "Quite a long time ago."

"Well, not that long ago."

"Just how long ago, Tom?"

Tom Watkins shifted his eyes. "I'm not that good on calendar time, to tell you the truth, Clara."

"What color was the pig you lost?"

"He was . . . well . . . he was kind of mud-colored."

They both looked into the pigpen. Willie was caked with mud from snout to tail, all four hoofs mired deep in a puddle.

"But, Clara," Tom went on, "Tod told me this was a big fat pig, and he's looking scrawny as a sick chicken. Are you feeding him right?"

"Of course I'm feeding him right! I take care of this pig like my own child."

"Still, maybe he'd do better over at my place, fatten up some before butchering time this fall. Especially if he turns out to be my pig."

"There's no way of knowing he's your pig, Tom."

"Clara, dear," Tom said, reaching for her hand, "maybe you'd do better over at my place, too. Did you ever think that this could be *our* pig?"

Clara's hand disappeared into her apron pocket. "*As I was saying,* Tom, there's no way of knowing it's your pig."

"Well, we know for a fact, Clara, that I lost a pig and you found one."

"We know that I found one."

"Clara Tolliver, are you saying I'm lying?"

"I'm saying just what I said. Till you can prove for a fact that this pig is yours, he's staying right here in this pen."

"We'll see about that. There's witnesses to my pig!"

"Well, you go round them up, and we'll hear what they have to say in a court of law. Now, if you'll excuse me . . ." Mama turned her back and marched off to the house.

"Tod Watkins is the court of law around here, Clara, and I think he's going to see eye to eye with me on this," Tom called after her. Then he turned back around, watching Willie's head droop dejectedly toward the puddle, and said in a satisfied way, "You're headed for my kitchen, pig, and that's a promise."

Maybelle and Louise sat where they had been sitting without saying a word for some time. Maybelle stared out one window, and Louise out the other. It was a good thing, thought Louise, that there were two windows, so they could look in different directions. Presently, however, there came a banging from Mama's bedroom next door, as if a bucket was being chased around the room.

"What's that noise, Louise?" asked Maybelle.

"Just somebody visiting, is all."

"Who would that be?" Maybelle asked suspiciously.

"Nobody you know, Maybelle, just one of Mama's long-lost relatives."

"How come you didn't introduce us?"

"She's a very shy relative."

"She doesn't sound shy. She sounds like she's about to tear the house down."

"That's just her way. Dear old Delilah. She loves the sound of that bucket, I mean racket, she makes a lot of racket when she moves around the room."

"I'll say! It sounds like she's . . ."

There was a crash against Mama's bedroom door and a grunting noise, *unh, unh unh*.

"Louise, something fishy's going on here."

"Not exactly fishy," said Louise, "but there is something going on. Maybe you heard we found a pig recently."

"I did hear that. So what?"

"It's a special pig, Maybelle, that's what I wanted to tell you about."

Maybelle swiveled her eyes around. "I don't care about that pig, Louise, and I'm not going to beat around the bush. I've got a question to ask you."

"Shoot, Maybelle."

"What in the world happened to your brother? I haven't seen him for a month of Sundays, and Uncle

Tod says he went off somewhere. You don't by any chance have him locked up in that room, do you?"

"Of course not! What are you trying to say, Maybelle?"

"What do you mean, what am I trying to say? I'm saying just what I said. Where is your brother?"

"Well, Mama told your uncle Tod that he might have gone to join the army, but like I've been trying to tell you, the day he left, this strange pig appeared, and we—"

"That boy's not old enough to join the army and, anyway, why wouldn't he tell you-all where he was going? Or at least tell me!"

"Maybelle, are you saying you're sweet on my brother?"

Maybelle turned from pig-snout-pink to rotten-tomato-red. "Louise Tolliver, I'm not saying anything except WHERE IS WILLIE?"

"It's hard to explain, Maybelle. As a matter of fact, it's sort of a surprise. If you'd just come on out to the pigpen, I can—"

"Why in the world would I want to see your old pig?"

"He's a real sweet pig, Maybelle. I've never known a pig quite like him."

Maybelle looked at Louise strangely.

"I mean . . . well, just trust me. You'll be glad you did."

"I'm getting real tired of hearing about this pig, Louise. I may have to look at him just so you'll shut up about it."

"Come on, then."

"Not now. I've got my best white shoes on. Anyway, here comes Daddy hollering for me. He thinks that pig belongs to him, by the way. Good-bye, Louise, and you better tell me if you hear from that brother of yours. He's going to be in big trouble with me, I can tell you that right now."

Maybelle rose to her white patent-leather-shoed feet and stalked majestically across the threshold, through the living room, and out the front door. Louise followed her and plunked down beside Mama on the porch swing. They watched Maybelle climb into the yellow truck holding her skirt up so it wouldn't get muddy on the running board.

"Maybelle's not going to listen to reason, Mama. We're going to have to trick her into kissing Willie."

"Tom, too," said Mama. "I mean, not into kissing Willie but into not killing him! Tom and Tod Watkins are going to get together on this thing, I can smell it coming." And Mama wrinkled up her nose like she smelled something bad.

CHAPTER 11

A Lullaby

The warm dark was full of fireflies. Mama and Louise sat on an old stump listening to the pine trees breathe. Molly Cow rested on the ground nearby, her legs folded under her. The shoats were fed but fretful.

"They sure want their mama back," Louise said sadly.

"Babies need a good snuggle to settle down for the night."

"Too bad Willie won't let them cuddle up to him."

Willie, who was leaning against the gate, backed away to the other side of the pen. Then he turned his head toward the woods.

"Well, it wouldn't be the same, anyway." Mama sighed.

"You reckon these babies would settle down if we sang to them?"

"It wouldn't hurt to try."

"Sing that old song you used to sing to me, Mama, when I yelled my head off because I didn't want to go to bed."

Mama started to sing, and Molly Cow moo'd like she always did when Mama sang. Even the shoats quieted down to a squeak while Mama rocked back and forth on the stump.

> Hush, little baby, don't say a word,
> Daddy's going to buy you a mockingbird.
> If that mockingbird don't sing,
> Daddy's going to buy you a diamond ring.
> If that diamond ring turns brass,
> Daddy's going to buy you a looking glass.
> If that looking glass gets broke,
> Daddy's going to buy you a billy goat.
> If that billy goat don't pull,
> Daddy's going to buy you a cart and bull.
> If that cart and bull turn over,
> Daddy's going to buy you a dog named Rover.
> If that dog named Rover don't bark,
> Daddy's going to buy you a horse and cart.
> If that horse and cart fall down,
> You'll still be the prettiest little baby in town.

"Sing it again, Mama," whispered Louise. "If you sing it over and over, it makes a circle."

"Most things do," said Mama. She sang the song again, and again.

By the time Mama finished singing the song three times, Louise was snuggled close beside her. Willie had moved over by the little shoats, who piled into a heap as near to him as possible. And huddled close to the fence was Delilah, a tear sparkling down her cheek in the starlight. The clearing stayed hushed for a long time.

Finally the owl *whoo'd,* and Louise peered up at Mama. "How come the song says Daddy's going to buy all that stuff, Mama? Daddy never bought us anything."

"He would have, honey, if he had been here."

"Well, where did he go, anyway?"

"I've told you a million times that I don't know, Louise."

"Folks say he ran off and left us."

"Folks say a lot of things they don't really know."

"But you don't know, either, Mama."

"I know that Jack Tolliver loved his wife and children. Whatever happened couldn't change that. But he was a dreamer, your daddy. He'd forget what he was doing smack dab in the middle of doing it."

"How come?"

"I don't know. It's just the way he was. He'd go out to milk Molly Cow and be standing there an hour later looking out the barn door at the sunset, just like you, Louise. I'd have to go bring him in for supper. But he had a pure-gold heart, and he could charm the birds down off the trees. Especially owls. The hoot owls used to visit every night. They sat there in plain sight—seemed like they were just about friends. And he could make things grow like magic. One minute there'd be little bean sprouts and the next, there'd be beans. I never knew what was going to happen next. Every single day with your daddy was full of surprises."

"Till he left."

"Well, that was quite a surprise, too, but it was a long time ago. I have two good children to keep me company, and life could be worse."

"Seems to me it *is* getting worse. Now you've only got one good child and one depressed pig."

"Well, you never know," said Mama. "Tomorrow is always a surprise."

"I'll say," said Louise.

"Tomorrow is also Sunday, and we have to get up early for church. It's time we went to bed."

"Did I really yell my head off at bedtime?"

"You did. Your head rolled right off on the floor."

"It did not."

"Sure, it did. Daddy had to run after it and put it back on again."

"He did not. Stop teasing."

"All right. Your daddy was magic, but not that magic. You better put Molly Cow in the barn, Louise. And help me get Delilah inside."

But Delilah would not come. Even with Mama taking one arm and Louise the other, Delilah would not budge. She set her feet in the ground and dug in. When Louise and Mama tried to pull her along, she yelled her head off.

"I guess we can't drag her in against her will," Mama said finally.

"Maybe you could sing again."

"She'd just settle down right here."

"Well, it's a nice night, now it's not raining. She'll be all right, Mama."

"I guess," said Mama. "But it doesn't seem right to leave her out here by herself."

"She's not by herself. She's got Willie and the shoats right nearby, and Mollie Cow in the barn, and the hoot owl hiding in the trees, and the fireflies all around, and the stars up above."

"She better watch out for those stars," said Mama.

"I'll say," said Louise.

CHAPTER 12

Luke Watkins

By the time Mama and Louise fed the shoats and walked all the way down the mountain to church, folks were already singing the first hymn. Mama pulled the door open, and Louise slipped in behind her. Not a single seat was left in the back rows. They had to march all the way down the aisle and file into a pew with Tom Watkins's family sitting right behind them. First in line was Maybelle, with every curl in place, then her brother Luke, with his curls sticking out every which way. Next to him sat Tom Watkins, with not much hair at all. On the other side of the church sat Tod Watkins, also without much hair. Up in the pulpit, Reverend Dan's deep voice was rolling along like a river to the sea. He had a full beard, and hair sprouting from his head, eyebrows, ears, nose, neck, and arms. His wife, Loretta, was banging away on the piano. She wore a hat that covered up her hair with bird feathers.

As Louise stood there waiting for the song to be over, she suddenly felt a sharp jab in her back. She whirled around and practically banged heads with Luke Watkins, pointing the corner of his hymnbook straight at Louise's spine and grinning like a fool. Louise made a face at him and turned back around.

Usually on a warm summer Sunday morning, Louise went halfway to sleep during church, starting with the silent prayer right before the sermon. But she was hungry today because she and Mama hadn't had time to eat breakfast. As soon as Reverend Dan called for silent prayer and the church got quiet, Louise heard her stomach give a monstrous growl. It sounded like a lion turned loose after starving in a cage for seven days and seven nights. And right after it came a snicker from Luke, followed by a yelp as Maybelle pinched him. Then Louise's stomach growled even louder, and Luke had a coughing fit. Louise could feel Maybelle's frown boring a hole in her back, right next to where Luke had jabbed her with the book. She also felt a tickling along her backbone.

After that, Louise could not get comfortable. While Reverend Dan preached, her back itched like it was crawling with spiders.

Reverend Dan's sermon was about helping yourself instead of expecting the Lord to do everything. "The Lord helps those who help themselves," said Reverend Dan. In fact, he said it quite a few too many times.

Louise tried to help herself by scratching her back, first with one hand and then with the other.

"Stop squirming, Louise," whispered Mama.

Louise sat still for a few minutes and then felt itchy again. She rubbed her back against the pew. The buttons made a clicking noise against the wood. There was another snicker from behind her, another yelp, and a loud, "SHHHH!" Reverend Dan's eyes seemed to bore right through her to a point behind, where Luke Watkins was sitting. Mama put her hand on Louise's knee to settle her down. Between the growling and the itching and the scratching and the clicking and the snickering and the yelping, Louise hardly heard a word Reverend Dan said, and she didn't get halfway to sleep, either. When the last hymn was finally over, everybody stood up to go, but Louise refused to turn around. She kept her eyes on the ground and waited while the back aisles emptied.

"Clara, you're looking fine today," said Tom Watkins. He reached out to shake Mama's hand and held it just a little bit too long. Mama pulled it back.

"Hello, Mrs. Tolliver," Maybelle said to Mama. "I know you're planning to bring a little something for the church table at the Labor Day picnic?"

"She's got an extra pig," said Tom. "She could bring that."

"I was thinking along the lines of chocolate cake, Tom," said Mama.

"Yumm!" shouted Luke.

"Hush up, you little beast," said Maybelle.

Louise finally looked up, trying to decide which one she didn't like more, Luke or Maybelle.

"How'd you like those hairy caterpillars I dropped down your back, Louise?" asked Luke.

"You did no such thing, liar," said Louise.

"How come you were wiggling around so much, then? They must be all squashed by now."

Louise clamped her mouth shut and looked down at the ground again. She guessed maybe she didn't like Luke more than she didn't like Maybelle. Unfortunately he was in her class at school, whereas Maybelle was in Willie's.

Finally it was the Watkinses' turn to file down the aisle and out the door. Mama and Louise followed along behind them and then turned toward the mountain. Old Giant simmered in the sunshine, and lunch was calling, "Hurry up, hurry up, hurry up." They were just about far enough away from the church that Louise could ask Mama to look down the back of her dress for squashed hairy caterpillars, when they heard someone hollering after them.

Mama squinted her eyes against the sun. "Tod?" she called out to the sheriff. "For pity's sake, slow down or you're going to fall down."

"Well, I had to catch up with you, Clara. I was talking to Tom, and he says the new pig that wandered into your yard is looking mighty sickly. I was just wanting to make sure you wouldn't let me take it off your hands and fatten it up some, compliments of the county."

"We already discussed that, Tod, and I said no, if you'll recall."

"Well, a woman can change her mind, can't she?"

"Not this woman," Mama said, "about this pig."

"Keep an open mind, Clara, is all I'm saying."

"My mind is open, but the subject is closed," said Mama.

"Tom doesn't think so. He still claims that pig is his."

"Do tell," said Mama.

"He says he has witnesses."

"Just how many people do you suppose could have seen his pig run away?" asked Mama. "We're in a hurry to get home now, Tod, if you don't mind. There's a lot to do, and like Reverend Dan just told us, the Lord helps those who help themselves."

"Speaking of help, I bet you could use some help around your place. Have you had any word from that boy of yours?"

"Not yet, but I'm sure he'll turn up soon."

"You let me know, hear? And if there's anything I can do for you meanwhile . . ."

"Good-bye, Tod."

As soon as they were out of hearing distance, Louise made Mama stop and look down the back of her dress.

"Well, no wonder you were wiggling, Louise, there's pine needles down your back. How in the world did they get there?"

"Luke Watkins is how."

"Well, it looks like you got yourself a boyfriend."

"Boyfriend! Mama, he just put pine needles down my back and told me it was hairy caterpillars."

"That's a sure sign," said Mama.

"Well, if that's a boyfriend, I'd rather have a pig."

"Watch out what you say, now, Louise. We've got

enough wishing and switching going on around here to last us a lifetime." Mama unbuttoned the back of Louise's dress, brushed off the pine needles, and buttoned her back up again. Then they hurried up the mountain to feed themselves and the hungry little shoats.

CHAPTER 13

Twins

Tom Watkins walked into Sheriff Tod Watkins's office and closed the door behind him. Tod Watkins, who had been taking an afternoon nap with his feet propped on the desk, sat up quickly and stared at his twin. "Brother Tom!"

"Brother Tod."

"What brings you here?"

"I've come on official business, about that runaway pig over at Clara Tolliver's place."

"I've already tried to talk her out of that pig. She's one hardheaded woman—hard-hearted, too, if you ask me."

"Nobody asked you about her heart. That's for me to take care of."

"You already had a wife, Tom. Now it's my turn."

"Tillie died three years ago, Tod, in case you don't recall. And with Willie gone, I've got a lot better chance of courting Clara. She's going to need a man around that place."

"Clara wouldn't marry you now any more than she would in the old days, Tom. She's still stuck on Jack Tolliver, always was and always will be. And don't forget she's still married to him, wherever he may be."

"Jack Tolliver has got to be either deader than a doornail or crazier than a loon to leave a woman pretty as Clara."

"Be that as it may, he did leave Clara, and I've got dibs on courting her, by right of being born before you by five full minutes."

"You just said yourself she wouldn't have another husband."

"I said she wouldn't have you, Tom, I didn't say anything about me. It's just possible that one of these days I could receive some kind of report on poor Jack Tolliver's demise in a faraway county. Then it would be my sad duty to inform the widow and comfort her afterward."

"Blast you, Tod, I didn't come here to fight about Clara Tolliver. I came to file a charge against her for stealing my pig."

"Maybe we can work together on this, Tom. At the first stage, anyway. If Clara Tolliver were to be convicted of theft and fined a large amount of money—which she does not have—or else face jail, she'd be in trouble. That could even leave her poor, remaining child Louise in an orphanage, something Clara would never stand for. Now it so happens that you and I have enough money. If marrying one of us were the only way to save her situation, she just might do it. After that, may the best man win. We could celebrate the wedding with a barbecue picnic on Labor Day."

"What she won't do out of love or greed, she might do out of need," said Tom.

"This woman has kept us apart for too long. Let's settle her once and for all, so we can settle ourselves."

"Brother Tod!"

"Brother Tom."

"I formally file charges against Clara Tolliver for stealing my pig."

"You mean *Widow* Tolliver. Poor little lady, she's getting two pieces of bad news at once—your charge of theft, and that report I just got on Jack Tolliver's demise in a faraway county."

CHAPTER 14

Search and Rescue

"Wake up, Willie, time for breakfast," Louise said, pouring the bucket of slops into the pig trough.

Willie was buried in mud. He did not move.

"Come on, Willie, stale biscuits with buttermilk— your favorite!"

The shoats swarmed near the fence where Louise stood. Willie lay still.

"Willie?" Louise set the bucket down. "Willie, look at me. Are you sick? Talk to me, Willie."

A cicada buzzed in the silence.

"Okay, don't talk, just grunt."

Several mud-bubbles popped in Willie's wallow.

Louise felt little fingers of fear creeping up the back of her neck. What if Willie had starved himself to death? She ran along the fence, fumbled with the latch, and pulled open the gate. Before she got halfway across the pigpen, Willie's mud puddle exploded. He leaped to his feet, streaked past Louise, charged through the open gateway, and headed for the woods. The shoats streamed after him and fanned out around the yard, squealing and screeching till Tollivers' Hollow echoed with pig panic. Louise stood in the middle of the pen, dazed and splattered with mud. She watched her mother running from the back door as if it were a bad dream. The shoats whirled around the yard, Mama whirled around after them, and the world whirled around like a fall wind full of leaves.

"Louise, don't just stand there!" yelled Mama. "Help me catch these pigs. Where's Willie?"

Louise looked up toward the top of Old Giant. "He got away, Mama. He took off up the mountain. I'll get him back." Then her legs seemed to come alive and run the same direction Willie ran, leaving Mama to tackle the shoats.

Louise dodged through the trees and flashed past the brambles. She had to find him. No telling what he would do. Willie was a desperate pig. He could stampede right off a cliff up there. He could get snakebitten, shot by a hunter, eaten by a mountain lion, or all three. And it was her fault. Twice her fault, first for changing him and second for letting him get away. Louise had never worried a single minute about Willie the boy, but Willie the pig was different. He was her responsibility. She was not just his sister anymore. She was in charge of him. She was Willie's human.

Louise's breath began to come in clumps. She was used to racing Willie the boy, and beating him. But she wasn't used to running for miles and miles up the mountain. On the other hand, neither was Willie. Maybe he was slowing down, too. She better keep her eyes open for tracks—and her ears open for heavy breathing. She stopped suddenly on the pathway. All she could hear was herself panting like a dog on a hot day. Then she heard something else. A little rustle. "Willie?" she called softly.

There was no answer. A little rustle could be anything. It could be a mouse. Or it could be a snake. Or a mountain lion. Or a hunter. Or Willie. Whatever it was, it was likely to be more scared of her than she was of it, except for hunters. You could never tell with hunters. Some of them would shoot anything that moved and figure out what it was later. Louise had a sudden picture of herself and Willie, stretched out on the ground, dead as doornails. Poor Mama.

"Willie?" she called again. "Where are you? Please, Willie, pretty please. I've figured out a plan to change you back. I told Mama about it this morning. I was coming out to tell you, too. Willie, are you there?"

There was another little rustle, farther away this time. Louise followed it. "Willie, you can't hide forever. Something bad could happen to you up here. I mean, something worse could happen to you."

One minute, Louise was standing at the edge of a briar patch, talking to thin air. The next minute she was talking to the tail end of a pig, which was backing out the other side of the briar patch. The briars were too thick for Louise to get through, so she ran around them. Willie ran, too.

"Stop! Willie, if you'd just listen. . . ." Louise was talking to thin air again, but she was headed the right way. She could hear the sounds of a frantic pig crashing through the underbrush ahead. Willie wasn't thinking anymore—he could have hidden in that briar patch for hours and she never would have found him. They were a long way from home, and Louise didn't know this part of the mountain. There were caves up here, and hollow trees to hide in. Losing Willie would be too easy. Louise couldn't bear to think about it. Instead, she kept shouting. "Willie, wait up. Let me talk to you. Willie, you're going to break Mama's heart running away like this."

There was a huge thud, and then there was Willie.

Louise almost fell over him. He was standing in an overgrown garden beside an old cabin, shaking his head. Maybe he had run into a wall. The walls were covered with vines—and with something else, too. Someone had painted circles with marks around them, nearly erased by years of wind and rain. She could not read the marks, but she could see the shapes. And she could also see that Willie had run as far as he could. His sides were heaving, his head was weaving, and his mouth was foaming.

This time Louise stood still. No sudden moves. Willie was like a wild boar now. He pawed the earth with a sharp hoof and hunched his body for a charge at this creature that had chased and trapped him. Louise opened her mouth to speak, but Willie was beyond words. So she began to hum, softly at first, hardly daring to breathe. After she hummed for a while, she sang, and she swayed as she sang.

> Hush little baby, don't say a word,
> Daddy's going to buy you a mockingbird.
> If that mockingbird don't sing,
> Daddy's going to buy you a diamond ring. . . .

Willie's eyes glazed over and his head swayed with her, back and forth, back and forth. Louise sang the song three times, singing a soothing circle around them. Then she turned around, slowly, slowly, and started to walk away. As she walked she talked, softly, softly, in a low, humming tone. "Let's go home, Willie, we need you at home. You can help Mama find the little lost shoats. They'll die on the mountain alone. Come along, Willie, it's time to go home."

Louise was afraid to look back, but she could listen. First she heard nothing. Then she heard a twig snapping behind her, and leaves rustling. One slow step after another, she hummed Willie down the mountain. They left the rocky shape of Old Giant lying above and the painted circles growing fainter behind. When Louise finally looked over her shoulder, she saw not a wild boar but a tired pig with drooping ears. His head hung low, and his tongue hung out. When she stopped to rest, he stepped up and leaned his head against her. She draped her arm around his muddy neck and sat quiet.

Then they walked toward Tollivers' Hollow together, side by side.

That night Mama came into Louise's room and sat down on the bed. Louise grabbed her hand. "Mama?"

"What?"

"We almost lost Willie today."

"I know it, Louise. You were lucky to find him."

"No, I don't mean that kind of lost. I mean he was all animal for a while, and I wasn't sure he was coming back. Not just coming back home, but coming back to his senses—his human senses."

"Thank goodness you found a way to remind him of who he is."

"And I found something else, Mama, a strange old house. It had circles painted all over it."

"Sadie Tolliver's, I bet. She was distant kin to your daddy. Sadie lived way back in the woods near the top of Old Giant, and dug herbs. She supposedly talked to owls, too, come to think of it—some people say there's a strange streak in your daddy's family. Anyway, Sadie died a long time ago. I never met her myself, but I heard about her. When people asked her for spells, she would draw circles with numbers around them. I guess that was supposed to mean something."

"Magic?"

"Maybe."

"I wish we had some of her magic."

"Well, we'll keep our fingers crossed. That's about as close to magic as I can get."

"I don't know, Mama, getting all those shoats back into the pigpen was pretty magical."

"That was just hard work and mud, Louise. I felt like I was at the county fair back in the old days. We used to have this contest, chasing a greased pig. Whoever caught the pig got the blue ribbon. I won three years in a row. I was pretty quick, back then, and I guess I haven't lost my touch."

"You got all but that last little shoat."

"We never would have found him except for Willie. Willie just knew where to look, and that little pig followed him right on back into the pen like a puppy."

"Willie's turning truly pig. How did Delilah do?"

"She ran around in circles and fell all over her feet. Poor Delilah, she's worn out and sound asleep, out there by the fence. I couldn't get her inside for love or money."

"We sure have to do something about this situation."

"We sure do."

Whoooo.

Louise and Mama looked out the window toward the pigpen and saw a dark shape swooping onto a branch of the big pine tree.

Moooo, Molly Cow called from the barn.

"Sounds like we got some agreement on that score," said Mama.

"Sounds like," said Louise.

CHAPTER 15

Spells

"I declare, Louise, you've got a greener thumb than your daddy. Those beans you helped me plant look like they're growing straight up to the top of Old Giant." Mama leaned back on her hoe and looked up at the tall stakes with leafy vines wound around them.

"Just like Jack and the Beanstalk," said Louise. "We could use a gold harp about now. I've been thinking again, Mama, what kind of magic is there besides wishes and kisses that can change things?" Louise jerked up a deep-rooted weed and threw it onto the pile at the end of her row.

"Well, there's that old story where the princess gets mad at the frog for following her home, even though she promised to marry him just to get her gold ball back from down the well. There he is, all slimy green on her nice white pillow, and she picks him up and throws him against the wall and, squash, he turns into a prince. But I'd hate to think how mean it would be to throw Willie against a wall."

"Even if we could."

"Yes, even if we could. He's a fairly hefty pig. I expect frogs squash easier than pigs."

"Probably hitting him over the head with a hammer wouldn't be the same."

"Probably not. And risky."

"So squashing is out. What else, then, besides wishes and kisses?"

Mama looked up at the cool clouds half covering the hot sun. "Well, spells, I guess."

"Don't you know any spells?"

"Nope, not me. Like I said, the only person who ever did spells around here was Sadie Tolliver." Mama paused for a minute and looked out over the garden.

Louise kept weeding, and Mama went back to hoeing. CHUNK, went the edge of the hoe on the ground. CHUNK, CHUNK, CHUNK. Wishes, CHUNK, kisses, CHUNK, spells, CHUNK CHUNK. It might take all three. Louise wished she knew some spells, CHUNK, CHUNK, CHUNK. She thought about the princess and the frog story. It didn't seem fair, somehow, that such a mean, selfish princess had gotten a prince. But maybe that's what she deserved, a smashed-frog prince. Who knew what kind of person *he* would be? Anyway, fairy tales weren't always fair. Jack stole the giant's harp and magic goose and bag of gold and then killed him, chopping down that beanstalk. And who knows what happened to the giant's wife? Of course, the giant ate people, but then, people ate pigs. It all depended on your point of view, whether you were eating or being eaten. Still, that story seemed a little out of kilter somehow.

And what happened to the cow, the faithful old family cow that Jack had swapped off for the magic beans? And whatever happened to the other bean seeds? And all that stuff Jack stole? The harp strings probably broke, and the goose that laid the golden eggs passed on. People spent the golden eggs, one by one, for this thing or that thing. The bag of gold, too, for this thing or that thing. Personally, Louise would rather have a cow. She looked over at Molly Cow, grazing in the field. You could count on a cow. A good cow gave you love and enough milk to live on. What more did you need?

Well, Louise needed a magic spell.

Meanwhile, she just kept weeding, and Mama kept hoeing. CHUNK, went the edge of the hoe on the ground. CHUNK, CHUNK, CHUNK. Wishes, CHUNK, kisses, CHUNK, spells, CHUNK CHUNK. It might take all three. Louise wished she knew some spells, CHUNK, CHUNK, CHUNK.

"One thing, Willie," said Louise, "if we ever get you out of this mess and you do get married to Maybelle, you're going to be the best daddy in the world. There's nothing like baby pigs to practice on."

The littlest shoat had gotten stuck trying to squeeze through the fence, and Willie was nosing it sideways to help it get unstuck. There was a good deal of squealing and grunting going on. Louise was just about to reach down and help when the piglet popped out and turned a backward somersault right into Willie's snout.

"Uuuuch!" Willie said loudly.

"Ouch, not uuuuch," said Louise. "Say it right, Willie."

Willie refused to say it right. He wandered over to the mud hole with the little shoat trotting after him.

"That shoat follows you around just like Maybelle used to," said Louise.

Louise watched Willie and the shoat circle around in the mud, leaving hoofprints to fill up with water. Big tracks, little tracks, around and around in a circle.

How did Sadie Tolliver make spells out of circles and numbers? The only circle Louise knew with numbers around it was a clock. She picked up a stick and began dabbling in the dirt. First she drew a circle. On top of the circle she wrote her name, Louise, just above where the 12 on a clock would be. It seemed like she had started this whole problem and, anyway, she'd be twelve on her next birthday. Next she wrote Willie's name, about 1:30 on the clock. Willie had been the first change. Then she wrote Delilah's name, about 3 o'clock. Delilah had been the second change. Then she stopped for a long time and looked up at the sun circling the sky.

When she looked down again, she wrote her daddy's name, Jack, about 4:30. There must have been some kind of change with her daddy, maybe a change of heart, despite what her mother said about him. Willie, Delilah, Jack, three changes of one kind or another. Down at the bottom, about 6 o'clock, she wrote Maybelle. Maybelle might help if they could figure out how to make her do it. And maybe Luke fit in there somewhere. She wasn't sure where, but since he was Maybelle's brother, she put his name at 7:30, near Maybelle's. Who else? Sheriff Tod Watkins didn't amount to much, and neither did Tom, but maybe together they added up. Somehow the Watkins family and the Tolliver family seemed linked up, for better or for worse. She put TomTod at 9 o'clock. And Louise wrote Mama about 10:30, up by her own name, which was comforting.

She studied this circle for a while. Then she drew a line from each name to its opposite name, from Louise to Maybelle, Willie to Luke, Delilah to Tom-Tod, Jack to Mama. Now instead of a clock it looked like a wheel. The middle of the wheel, where the lines all crossed, made a star connected to everybody. Louise, Willie, Delilah, Jack, Maybelle, Luke, TomTod, Mama, Star—ten creatures of one kind or another, all circle-bound one way or the other. All in pairs except

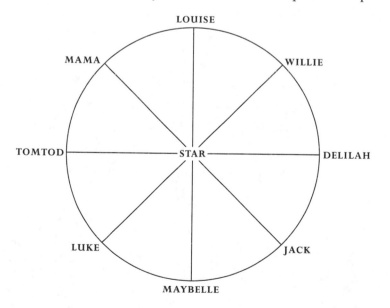

for the star, though she surely never thought of herself paired with Maybelle. Oh, well, they were both girls. Willie and Luke were both boys. Jack and Mama belonged together, even though they'd been apart for so long. That left Delilah and TomTod. Underneath the way they looked, there might be some real resemblance. None of them seemed too bright. Of course, Delilah had not had the advantage of being human very long.

Louise peered at the drawing while the sun went down. She didn't know what it meant, but it looked right and it settled in her mind. She was so deep in the circle that she practically jumped out of her skin when something swooshed close over her head. There came the familiar eerie sound from up in the trees— *whoo-whoo, whoo-whoo.*

"WHO is right!" Louise shouted, throwing her head back. "Who the heck scared me out of my wits?" She glared up at the trees.

A big hoot owl stared back down at her, clear as daylight, beak clicking and yellow eyes forming a circle on each side of its head.

CHAPTER 16

Worries

"Mama! I saw that old owl out in the pine tree—the one we've been hearing all this time. He swooped down on me like I was mouse-meat."

"That's funny. The owls used to do that to your daddy. I think it's kind of a joke."

"Not for the mouse."

"I guess every kind of creature has its own ways," said Mama. "Jack used to tell me that owls knew a lot they weren't saying."

"I wish Willie would try to say things. What if he just turns totally pig, inside as well as outside?"

"Surely we'll figure out something before then."

"We've got to work fast, Mama. The Labor Day picnic is coming up soon, and Tom and Tod both want to barbecue Willie. If we manage to keep him safe past that, school starts and those truant officers will come up here looking for him. They're mostly not as dumb as Tod Watkins, plus they have all these reports to fill out and turn in and then who knows who-all will come sniffing around here looking for Willie. They're getting real strict about school, and Willie never missed any."

"One day at a time, Louise. In hard times you have to take one day at a time—in good times, too, come to think of it."

Delilah trotted into the kitchen, found the bucket empty, and began banging it against the stove.

"Delilah, don't bang the bucket. Say 'milk.' MILK, MILK.'"

Delilah looked at Louise and banged the bucket. Mama put her hands over her ears. "She hears the shoats squealing. You better go milk Molly Cow, Louise, it's late. We have to feed all these creatures."

Louise managed to take the bucket away from Delilah, who followed her out to the barn, lay down in the hay while Louise milked Molly Cow, ambled after her to the pigpen, and trotted around in anxious circles while Mama and Louise fed the shoats. The owl did not dive down again but stayed silent in the trees with his eyes closed. Mama hummed the mockingbird lullaby again.

"You know, Mama, those things in the song are all around us. We don't need anybody to buy them for us. We already have mockingbirds, and a pond we can see ourselves in but won't ever break like a looking glass. I guess Molly Cow is as good as any old dog named Rover, or billy goat, or bull."

"Better—she gives us so much milk."

"And who needs a diamond ring, anyway?" asked Louise.

"Well, sometimes I think it wouldn't hurt to have a little something to sell, just in case."

"As long as we've all got each other, Mama, we don't need any money."

"Well, two of us are kind of missing."

Louise looked over at her brother, lolling in the mud. Willie looked pretty comfortable there, and she barely remembered her father enough to miss him. "I'm just trying to count our blessings, Mama. We've even got eleven little shoats!"

"So true," said Mama.

Whoo, said the owl.

"Howl," said Willie.

"Owl, Willie," said Louise. "Say 'owl,' not 'howl.'"

"Howl," said Willie.

"Hopeless," said Louise. "Anyway, we've got Molly Cow and a Tolliver owl. It just about rhymes."

Whoo, click-click, said the owl.

"Sounds like he's trying to talk to us, Mama."

"All I hear is 'who.' Maybe you can figure it out, Louise. Your daddy could have. You look so much like your daddy right now. His hair used to turn red in the sun like that, and dark at night. His eyes, too, were kind of in between. Hazel eyes. They looked green in the light and brown at night. Between day and night, with the sun going down like it is right now, he just glowed. Like that owl there."

Louise looked up at the owl. Its feathers had a light and dark pattern lit up by a ray from the setting sun. Louise watched the pattern fade as twilight slipped into darkness. Evening was Louise's favorite time of day. But what did evening mean? Did it mean making things even? Evening things out? Getting even? Or just balancing day and night, evening odd things? And did odd mean different, like even and odd numbers, or did odd mean strange, like the Tollivers? How did you even odd things out?

That night she saw the owl in her dreams. It was not saying *whoo-whoo* but *how-how.* The owl had its head turned, so she could see only one eye, but the eye was a big circle that spun around. There was a star in the middle and names all around, just like the one Louise had drawn in the dirt. With the circle spinning, sometimes Louise's name was on top, sometimes at the bottom, but the same names stayed across from each other, connected by lines from Louise to Maybelle, Willie to Luke, Delilah to TomTod, Jack to Mama. With the circle spinning and the star pulsing, Louise started to get dizzy. The circle wheeled around and around, she sailed to the top, and she swooped to the bottom. It was hard to hang on, halfway between heaven and Earth, halfway between day and night. Her hands began to sweat and slip a little each time she swooped down. On a last fast turn at the bottom of the circle, Louise's fingertips slipped off. Suddenly she was falling, falling, falling through several sunsets ablaze with red and yellow, falling down toward a mountain of rotten tomatoes.

CHAPTER 17

A Plan

"This is getting scarier and scarier, Mama. I don't know what-all it means," Louise said the next morning, after she told Mama about the dream.

"It's a mystery to me," said Mama. "I can't tell whether we're dealing with stars or wishes or kisses or spells."

"Maybe all three," said Louise. "Maybe the dream means we have to put all the magic together into one big bang."

"Seems to me the magic is getting a little out of hand around here," said Mama. "The cure might be worse than the sickness." Then she looked out the window at Willie and Delilah, each drooping on different sides of the pigpen fence. "But I guess not," she added, "if we can really fix things back the way they were."

"I don't know if things will ever be the way they were, Mama, but maybe we can fix them different."

"All I have to say is that's one mean star."

"Maybe the star's not too happy, either. I thought about that last night, with the star blinking away in the middle of the circle. Maybe that wish I made, without really meaning to make it, kind of knocked things out of kilter. Or maybe they've been a little bit out of kilter for a while and I knocked them the rest of the way. The star's part of it, though. We're all in this together some way."

"It would help to know which way that is."

"You know what the preacher said, Mama, and you said it, too. The Lord helps those who help themselves."

"We don't need a sermon here, Louise, we need some idea about what to do next."

"I'm getting to that, Mama. I'm thinking maybe I need to have a birthday party real soon."

"Your birthday's not for months!"

"I know that, but nobody else remembers it except maybe Doc Brady. We need to put together all the wishes, kisses, and spells we can muster for that one big magic bang. We need to get Maybelle to kiss

Willie. We need to get Tod—or else Tom, or maybe both—to kiss Delilah. We might need Luke, too, but I don't know what for yet. We need to do all this while the sun's going down and the first star's coming out with a new moon. And it wouldn't hurt to have a great big dirt drawing of that circle I told you about, too, which I will stand in the middle of to make one last wish. All before the Labor Day picnic."

"Lord have mercy, Louise, that's like trying to organize the Last Judgment. What am I supposed to do?"

"I don't know, Mama, but it sounds like there'll be plenty to help out with. You could sing the mockingbird song. That's kind of magic all by itself."

"And how do you know all this, may I ask?"

"I don't know that, either, Mama, I'm just trying to put things together. Do you think I knew what I was doing when I called Willie a pig? There's some kind of power loose around here. Who knows what's going to happen next?"

CHAPTER 18

An Invitation

"Should we start out with 'Dear Tom,' or 'Dear Tod,' or 'Dear Tom and Tod' so they can share it?" asked Louise.

"I hate to say 'Dear Tom *or* Dear Tod.' They might think I mean it," said Mama.

"And I hate to say 'Dear Maybelle.' She might think I mean it, too. Or 'Dear Luke,' ditto."

"Maybe we just better say 'Dear Friends.' That sounds kind of general. Then we can address one copy to Tod and another copy to Tom and Maybelle and Luke."

"All right, 'Dear Friends.' What next?" Louise stuck her tongue out. She always stuck her tongue out when she was writing something hard.

"'You are invited' sounds pretty good."

"'You are invited to celebrate Louise Tolliver's twelfth birthday.'"

"Will you really be twelve your next birthday, Louise Tolliver?"

"You should know, Mama, you birthed me."

"My goodness, child, how time flies."

"And owls. Come on, now, Mama, we have to get on with this letter."

They tried seven different ways to say the same thing. The words had to be just right to tell enough but not too much. Mama and Louise kept changing them around like a jigsaw puzzle. After they finished, Louise read the letter out loud:

Dear Friends,

You are invited to celebrate Louise Tolliver's twelfth birthday at a surprise party. This is a surprise because of the date, which nobody will know till it comes. On the first clear evening with a new moon, come to dinner at the Tollivers' before sunset. There is no need to bring gifts. Just bring yourselves. A lively time is guaranteed. Please RSVP.

> Yours truly,
> Clara and Louise Tolliver

"There, now, does that sound too mysterious?" asked Louise.

"Everybody likes a little mystery," said Mama.

"But not too much," said Louise.

"No, too much gets creepy. This is just right. They'll come."

"I sure hope so," said Louise.

"They'll think it's real strange, but Tom and Tod will come, anyway, to see me," said Mama. "Luke will come to see you, and Maybelle will come hoping someway to see Willie."

"We know Willie and Delilah will be here," said Louise.

Whoo-whoo, called the owl outside. "You don't reckon we need that old owl, do you?"

"That's up to you, Louise. I never did pretend to understand that owl."

"I think the owl understands more than both of us put together."

"That wouldn't be too hard."

"So now we wait for an answer?"

"And the first clear evening with a new moon."

CHAPTER 19

An Answer

The road that had been deep mud dried to deep dust. After Tod Watkins's red truck stopped in front of the house, all Louise and Mama could see was a big dusty cloud with a pair of bowlegs walking toward them.

"Keep shelling those peas, Louise. I think we're about to get an answer to our invitation," whispered Mama.

Louise and Mama both grabbed some more pea pods and pushed the squeaky porch swing back and forth with their feet.

After a while the dust settled, and Sheriff Watkins stood before them, shuffling his own feet. Every time he did, the dust raised a little cloud around each toe.

Sheriff Watkins coughed a little and cleared his

throat. "Howdy, Clara, always a pleasure to see you—looking pretty as ever. Louise."

"Hello, Tod," said Mama.

"Mr. Watkins," said Louise.

"Tom and I and Maybelle and Luke got your invitation."

"I'm glad," said Mama, "and I hope you'll all be here when the time comes."

"Wouldn't miss it for the world. It's not every day a little lady turns twelve."

"I'll say," said Louise. "Seems like it takes a whole year after she turns eleven."

Mama jabbed Louise in the ribs with her elbow.

"Just when is your birthday, anyway, Louise?" asked Sheriff Watkins.

"That's a secret, Tod," said Mama. "In a place like this, where everybody knows everybody else's business, a lady does well to keep her birthday to herself or by and by everybody will know how old she is at a time of life when she doesn't care for that fact to be known."

"I can see your point, there, Clara, though eleven years old—or twelve or whatever—seems a little young to be worrying about it. At any rate, we can all see for ourselves when the first clear evening with a new moon comes, and we'll be here for dinner before sunset, bringing no gifts except ourselves and hoping for a lively time like you guaranteed."

"You seem to have taken the invitation to heart, Tod—you practically *learned* it by heart," said Mama.

"You are a subject always close to my heart, Clara, as you well know."

"I hardly think that's an appropriate remark to make to a married woman, Tod Watkins."

"Well now, Clara, that raises another matter that I have to tell you about, and I can't put it off any longer. It's a sad business for me to relate, but this very morning I got word of Jack Tolliver's demise."

Mama went still. Her knucklebones turned white around the bright green pea pods crushed in her hand. Her pink cheeks turned white, too, and Louise could see the black circles under her eyes from getting up at night to feed the baby pigs.

"I don't believe it," Mama said finally.

"Why in the world not, Clara?" asked Tod Watkins.

"Because I would have felt it inside. I've known Jack was alive from the day he disappeared seven years ago, and somehow I'd know if he was dead. Where did you get this information, anyway? And how and where was he supposed to have died?"

"There weren't that many details, to tell you the truth, Clara, but I'll surely follow up on it and give you a full report of what's known."

"You do that, Tod. I'd like to see it in writing and signed by whoever sent it."

"Well now, speaking of writing and signing, there's one more thing, Clara, since I'm delivering bad news."

"And what might that be?"

"Tom has formally charged you with the theft of his pig."

"Tom Watkins is full of hot air."

"Clara, I feel it's my duty as a friend—"

"A friend of me or Tom?"

"You, of course, Clara, always you— to warn you that if you're found guilty, it would probably mean a big fine, or else jail."

"That's real friendly of you, Tod."

"I could be more than friendly, Clara, if you'd just let me. I could take care of that fine, for instance, and you wouldn't have to worry about little Miss Louise here going to the orphanage."

"What orphanage, Tod? What are you talking about?"

"Well now, Clara, I don't want to spell it all out too plain, but if you can't pay the fine and you have to spend some time in jail, Louise here would be left on her own, without Willie around. Being a minor and all, she couldn't very well stay by herself. But, like I say, you can count on me if you need some help out of this mess. A pretty widow like you doesn't have to spend her whole life alone with so many problems on her hands."

"First of all, you haven't proved to me that Jack is dead. Second of all, you haven't proved that I stole Tom's pig. Third of all, Willie may come back any day now. And fourth of all . . . fourth of all . . ."

"Fourth of all," said Louise, "I'd rather go to an orphanage than make Mama marry you, Mr. Watkins, with all due respect."

Sheriff Watkins stared down at his feet, which had stopped stirring up toe-clouds of dust. Finally he looked up at Mama and Louise. "We shall see what we shall see, ladies," he said solemnly. "Just think about my offer."

"We shall see you at the party, at any rate," said Mama. "No hard feelings, I hope?"

"My feelings for you, Clara, are always soft."

Louise made a little gagging sound, and Mama poked her in the ribs again.

"Good day, Clara, Louise."

"Good-bye, Tod," said Mama.

"Mr. Watkins." Louise nodded.

The dust had not settled before Tom Watkins's yellow truck showed up. He swung open the door and walked confidently up to the porch, sweeping his hat off to Mama and Louise on their porch swing. "Ladies!"

"Tom," said Mama.

"Mr. Watkins," said Louise.

"We received your invitation and would be delighted to come. I speak on behalf of myself, Maybelle, Luke, and Tod."

"Tod has already spoken on his own behalf," Mama said, "but thank you for letting us know, anyway."

"Tod's been here?"

"Just before you came."

"Maybe he's told you, then, about me having to file charges regarding that pig of mine that you're keeping here?"

"He didn't say you had to do it. He said you did it."

"Well now, Clara, I hope it doesn't come to anything in the end. You know, there's more than one way to skin a cat—or, in this case, a pig. Ha-ha."

"What do you mean by 'more than one way to skin a cat,' Tom? I've always found that to be a very unpleasant expression."

"What I mean is, I could be persuaded to drop charges, Clara. After all, you don't have money to pay a pig fine, I mean big fine—a big pig fine, ha-ha—and going to jail would leave poor little Louise here an orphan. So maybe we could come to some agreement."

"What kind of agreement do you have in mind, Tom?"

"Nothing I haven't suggested before, Clara, but

now it looks like you might be free to take me up on it, with Jack's demise. Tod told me the sad news."

"Tod told you before he told me? Well, we're not sad, because we don't believe it."

"You can believe I've filed charges."

"Yes, Tom, I can believe you've done that."

"No hard feelings, just trying to get things straightened out."

"No hard feelings. Louise and I are trying to straighten a few things out, too. Which reminds me, we'll count on you and the family for that birthday party."

"Right, Clara, a family affair. Just as it should be. All families have their little differences to straighten out. We'll be here with rings on our fingers and bells on our toes—isn't that what the old nursery rhyme says? My ring on your finger, if it was up to me."

"It's not up to you, Tom."

"We shall see what we shall see, ladies. Good day, Clara, Louise."

"Tom."

"Mr. Watkins."

Mama and Louise were quiet while Tom Watkins drove out of sight. Slowly each one picked up another pea pod. Then they looked at each other.

"What now, Mama?" asked Louise.

"I'm not completely sure, Louise. This strikes me as a tricky situation."

"Seems like it's getting trickier all the time."

"I wouldn't disagree with that," said Mama.

"Well, we got the answer to our invitation."

"And we're bound to get a clear evening with a new moon."

"Better sooner than later, what with all this bad news. Do you really think Daddy is alive?"

"There is no question in my mind. Well, there might be some question in my mind, but there is no question in my heart. However, I wouldn't mind having some proof one way or the other, at long last."

"And do you really think Tom would press charges and Tod would make you pay, or put you in jail and me in an orphanage?"

"I think Tom and Tod are smarter than I thought they were but not as smart as they think they are. They're just using jail and the orphanage to scare us, but they could make trouble, and it's true that we don't have any money to get out of it. We have to take this thing one day at a time, like I said, and try to keep our balance."

"Did they always want to marry you?"

"Ever since they turned old enough to think

about such things. And I always felt bad because it caused a falling-out between them and they'd been close as two peas in a pod." Mama snapped open a pod and popped out a row of peas that looked just alike.

"But you always wanted to marry Daddy."

"Every day of my life. And after I did, Tom went off and married Tillie Watkins and had Maybelle and Luke, and Tod swore to a single life, and I thought that would settle things between them. But they never did get back together like twin brothers should be. Seems like they just got knocked out of balance."

"Do you think there's a natural balance to things, Mama?"

"There's some kind of balance to things, and we have to find it. Or if there isn't one, we have to make it."

"But things keep changing."

"Yes, and we have to change with them. Tillie Watkins died, your daddy disappeared, Willie turned into a . . . well, Willie has certainly changed. Not to mention Delilah."

"And the owl appeared."

"Whatever that means," said Mama.

"Maybe some new kind of balance?" asked Louise.

"Could be," said Mama. "But let me tell you, balance doesn't come easy. You know that old log that fell across the creek? It's balanced there, all right, but you have to find your own balance walking on it—one step at a time."

"So I guess the next step is giving this party," said Louise.

"Easy as falling off a log."

CHAPTER 20

A New Circle

Louise did her best thinking while she was milking Molly Cow. She leaned forward and pulled on the udders, first one and then the other, with a nice, even rhythm. Molly Cow stood still and patient. The milk squirted into the bucket, squish-squish-squish, squish-squish-squish. Louise thought about wishes, kisses, spells, stars, songs, and pigs. Then she started all over again with wishes. That was the trickiest part. She thought they could manage the kisses, one way or the other. As for spells, the people-wheel spun around and around in Louise's mind night and day now, big as life and twice as natural. Making a spell was like Mama's Blue-Ribbon Chocolate Cake recipe. You took what you had and what you knew and what you felt and what you guessed and you mixed them all together, and remembered to look out the window and listen to the birds sing while you were doing it. Plus, it didn't hurt to count your blessings while you were beating the batter. Louise thought this might be the recipe for the whole world.

Stars, though, were a mystery. Stars were out of her range. It was pretty clear that Louise didn't have a clue about that star. She just had to feel her way along the dark ground of planet Earth and hope for the best. The song, on the other hand, was a sure thing. Mama was always a sure thing. As far as pigs went, well, the whole point of the big magic bang was to switch the pigs around—Willie and Delilah would be taken care of if she could just get the wishes right. She mulled over all kinds of different wishes, trying to pick the right one, the one to try for the big magic bang, the last wish left. If she got it wrong, there might not be another chance.

She needed to wish for Willie to turn human and Delilah to turn pig, but that might count as two wishes and only the first one would turn out. She had to put her brother first, didn't she? But then, poor Delilah. Maybe she could wish that everything in the pigpen would be turned back into its real self. But who knew what-all was in the pigpen? There could be creepy-crawly things that had been some kind of terrible outlaw killers in a former life. Louise wasn't so sure anymore of what she used to think she knew. And at the back of her mind was this little tiny wish, hiding in a briar patch of tangled-up thoughts, that she'd like to bring her daddy back. But what if her daddy was dead and suddenly his bones appeared on the front porch? That would just about kill Mama. Not to mention prove that Tom and Tod Watkins were right for once.

So never mind about Daddy. She just had to work out the right wish for Willie and Delilah. One thing at a time. The trouble was, there were two—two things at one time. The circle spun into Louise's mind. Two at one time.

Then she knew. The circle needed a few changes here and there. That's what was wrong. The thing about Mama's recipe was, it left room for changes here and there.

Now Louise knew exactly what to wish for.

She stood up and patted Molly Cow's bony rump. Molly Cow stretched her neck to look around at Louise.

"Thank you, Molly Cow," said Louise. "Thank you for this bucket of milk. Thank you for helping me think about wishes and kisses and spells and stars and pigs—but especially wishes. You are the best cow the world has ever known."

Molly Cow seemed to agree with this statement. She nuzzled Louise's ear and made a soft little sound with her lips, like a kiss. A cow kiss. Louise threw her arms around Molly Cow's neck and gave her a hug. A human hug. Then she walked up to the house with her bucket full of milk and her head full of wishes, kisses, spells, stars, songs, and pigs.

CHAPTER 21

Getting Ready

Mama and Louise watched anxiously as the beginning of August came with clear night skies. But the day of the new moon clouded over, and by evening rain was pouring down on the world, people and pigs both. The people huddled in their houses, and the pigs huddled in their mud, which was getting deeper by the minute. Louise lay in bed, looking out the window, her eyes as watery as the world outside. She had gotten everything ready for tonight, but tonight was not ready for her. The party would have to wait another whole month.

Mama came in to kiss her good night.

"This happened before, Mama, when I tried to make the second wish. It rained so hard, we couldn't even see the stars."

"Well, maybe the third time will be the right time."

"But this is such bad luck."

"Luck is what you make it, Louise. Maybe you need more time than you thought. Maybe another month will give you time to be even more ready."

"What if it rains every month, Mama? The party will never happen. We'll never be able to put things right again."

"It's not going to rain every night of the new moon for the rest of our lives, Louise."

"But time is running out, Mama. We have to change things before they get worse."

"We have to take . . ."

". . . one day at a time. I know, I know, but it's hard to wait any longer. Willie's getting way too thin for a pig, and Delilah's getting way too fat for a human, and Tod and Tom are trying to get you in trouble so you'll marry one of them, and folks are going to come looking for Willie after school starts, and we don't know what-all besides that."

"Goodness, Louise, you will never get to sleep thinking those troublesome thoughts."

"Sing to me, Mama."

So Mama sang. She sang "Hush Little Baby," and she sang "Amazing Grace," and she sang "Let the Circle Be Unbroken."

With an unbroken circle wheeling in her head,

Louise finally fell asleep. When she woke up next morning, a mockingbird was singing right outside the window where rain had been streaming down the night before. It was a good sign.

Thirty more days to get ready. There was a lot to remember.

"We need to put together all the wishes, kisses, and spells we can muster for that one big magic bang. We need to get Maybelle to kiss Willie. We need to get Tod—or else Tom, or maybe both—to kiss Delilah. We might need Luke, too, but I don't know what for yet. We need to do all this while the sun's going down and the first star's coming out with a new moon. And it wouldn't hurt to have a great big dirt drawing of that circle . . . which I will stand in the middle of to make one last wish. And Mama to sing the mockingbird song that's kind of magic all by itself.

All before the Labor Day picnic."

Louise went through every single step, every single day, over and over, for a whole month. Maybe it was a good thing Labor Day came late this year. It would give her almost an extra week.

September brought a wind that blew every cloud across the hills and out of sight. The morning of the new moon was clear as a mountain stream. Mama and Louise finished the cooking and baking they had worked on for two days.

"Did you count your blessings while you beat the batter?" Louise asked Mama.

Mama smiled. "I did my best, Louise, but I have to admit wishing maybe I'd have even more blessings to count the next time I make that cake."

They tidied up the house, dragged the table from the kitchen to the living room, and decorated it for the festivities. They tried to keep Delilah still while they buttoned on a new dress that Mama had made out of two of her old dresses sewed together. Delilah was getting truly hefty.

Louise went to bring Molly in from the pasture. The old cow stepped slowly along the path, as if she didn't want to come in. Louise pulled her along by one harp horn. Twice Molly Cow balked, and Louise had to go back and talk her into moving.

"What's wrong, Molly Cow? It's early for milking, but you don't mind, do you?" Louise stroked Molly Cow's fuzzy ears, which flicked back and forth like antennas, listening. Finally she took another slow step forward and moved toward the barn. After milking, Louise stood up and gave Molly one more hug. "I don't know what part you're going to play in this, Molly Cow, but be ready. We're going to need all the help we can get when the time comes."

Molly Cow lowered her head and leaned against the wooden stall. Louise left her like that, standing very still, and went to check on the pigpen. She brushed dried mud off Willie, threw a bucket of water over him, and rubbed his skin clean with a soft cloth. Willie looked puzzled, but he didn't say anything. Willie hadn't said anything for a long time except "Uhnk, uhnk, uhnk." He mostly lay in the pigpen looking thin and miserable while the little shoats, who were finally weaned, raced over to gobble all the slops in the trough.

Louise looked up into the tree. The owl perched there night and day now. Sometimes he flew off to catch a midnight snack, Mama said—which meant Mama was not sleeping too well herself—but he always came back.

Down the mountain on the other side of town, the Watkinses had been watching the moon, too. It looked like the time had come for a party.

Maybelle laid out her best dress and white shoes. On second thought, she swapped the white shoes for an older pair of black ones. The Tollivers' yard was bound to be either muddy or dusty.

Luke didn't do much of anything. He had forgotten all about the party till his father reminded him to wash his face.

Late in the afternoon Tom Watkins, looking spiffy,

herded Maybelle, looking very spiffy, and Luke, looking less than spiffy, into the yellow truck and headed
up to the Tollivers'.

About the same time, Tod Watkins, spiffed up as
much as possible, started his red truck and headed in
the same direction.

They arrived at the same time, nodded at each
other, and marched up to the house, where Mama and
Louise waited inside.

CHAPTER 22

The Party

"Happy Birthday, Louise," Maybelle said stiffly. She looked over at the table, set with eight plates.

"How come there's extra places at the table?" said Maybelle. "There's only six of us here, unless that brother of yours has come home."

"Well, you never know," said Louise. "We always set a place for Willie so he'll know he hasn't been forgotten, just in case he shows up at the door, which he hasn't yet but might any minute."

"And we do have another guest," Mama added quickly, "someone you-all haven't met yet, one of my long-lost relatives, named Delilah. She's quite shy, however."

"Shy but noisy, as I recall," said Maybelle. "I believe

I heard her banging around in your room the last time we visited."

"That's the one," said Louise. There was a resounding snore from Mama's bedroom.

"She sounds tired to me," said Tod.

"Delilah may or may not join us," said Mama, "depending on her mood."

Louise hoped that Delilah still had her dress on.

"Well now," said Tom Watkins, "I'm in a hungry mood right now, so how about if we eat?"

"Amen," said Tod.

Luke rubbed his stomach and patted his head at the same time, a trick he had been practicing for some time. It's not as easy at it looks, and he did it quite well, Louise thought.

"To tell you the truth, we're not quite ready to eat yet," said Mama.

"We were thinking we'd play some games first," said Louise.

"Games!" said Maybelle.

"What kind of games?" asked Tom. Tod's face reflected the same exact suspicion as Tom's.

"Party games, I bet," smirked Luke.

"Well, it is a party," said Mama.

"We thought we'd start out with blindman's buff," said Louise.

"Oh, brother," said Luke. "That's so easy. I always win at blindman's buff."

"Because you cheat," sniffed Maybelle.

"No cheating this time," said Louise. "If you peek, you lose. All you get is a punch in the nose."

"From who, you? I'm so scared," simpered Luke.

"Don't get into a fuss now," said Mama. "We're here to enjoy ourselves. Tom and Tod, have some elderberry wine to tide you over till suppertime. Maybelle and Luke, there's milk-and-honey on the side table. Louise, you go see if things are . . . um . . . ready, while I serve our guests." Mama twirled around the room in her best dress and long, fringed shawl.

Louise walked outside into the blessed cool of the evening. A brilliant red sunset was just beginning to fade. It wouldn't be long now. She picked up a stick and drew a big circle in the dirt. On top of the circle she wrote her name, Louise, just above where the 12 on a clock would be. Next she wrote Willie's name, at about 1 on the clock. At the 2 o'clock spot, she wrote Delilah. At the 3 o'clock spot, she wrote Jack. So far, the order was the same but the names were squished closer, because now she had to get in more names. That was the problem before, or at least one problem, with figuring out the right wish and fitting it with the spell. She had forgotten to put the animals in the circle. Animals were just as important as people, even if most people didn't think so. And even if the animals weren't exactly standing in the circle, their sounds would be there, considering that they hardly ever shut up. At the 4 o'clock spot she wrote Molly Cow. At 5 o'clock she wrote Tom. At 6 she wrote Luke, and at 7 Maybelle. At 8 she wrote Shoats, at 9 Clara (she had better use Mama's name since there was more than one mother), at 10 Tolliver Owl, and at 11 Tod.

Now she drew the lines between them. Louise at 12 to, ugh, Luke at 6, but it had to be that way so that Willie, who came next at 1, got paired off with Maybelle at 7. She drew a line between Delilah at 2 and

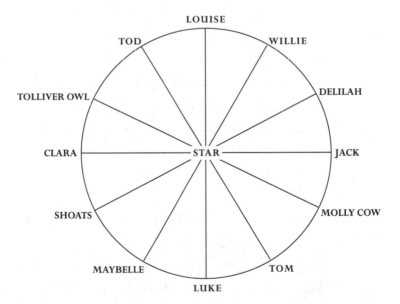

Shoats at 8, then between Jack at 3 and Clara at 9, Molly Cow at 4 and Tolliver Owl at 10. Finally, she drew the last line between Tom at 5 and Tod at 11. That had been Louise's other mistake, not to see the right pairs. No wonder everything was out of balance. In her heart, though, Louise felt like things had been out of balance for a long time, and it wasn't all her fault. In the circle, those who belonged together were connected. The middle of the wheel, where the lines all crossed, still made a star joining everybody. Louise and Luke; Willie and Maybelle; Delilah and the Shoats; Jack and Clara; Molly Cow and the Tolliver Owl; Tom and Tod; and the star by itself in the middle—13 creatures (23 if you counted every shoat) of one kind or another, all circle-bound one way or the other.

Suddenly, from right behind her, came a shrill voice. "What in the world are you doing, Louise Tolliver?"

Louise jumped back. Maybelle was practically breathing in her ear. "Just getting ready," said Louise.

"For what? I thought we were going to play blind-man's buff."

"Uh, this is a new kind of hopscotch, Maybelle. I just thought I'd set it up for later."

"Honestly, Louise, this is all baby stuff. You're supposed to be turning 12 years old. Last time I visited, you and your mother were playing dolls. Something's wrong with you Tollivers."

"Willie seemed to please you well enough."

"When he's around. There's something wrong with Willie, too, disappearing like he's done."

Just then Mama came to the door with several big white handkerchiefs dangling from her hands.

"Time to get started," she called anxiously to Louise, "before it gets too dark out here." Tod, Tom, and Luke trailed after her out onto the porch and down the steps.

"You're going to have to remind me of the rules," said Tod. "It's been a long time since I played blindman's buff."

Luke snickered. Tod had drunk quite a bit of elderberry wine and was not entirely steady on his feet.

"Actually, Louise suggested revising the rules somewhat," said Mama. "Usually one person is "It" and has to wear the blindfold and then tag somebody else in the group, and then that person is It. We thought it would be fun if we sort of divided the group in two, half It and half free. Maybe starting out with the Watkinses— Tod, Tom, Maybelle, and Luke—being It, and the Tollivers—Louise, Delilah, and me—being free."

"How about starting out with the Tollivers being It and the Watkinses being free?" said Tom.

"That wouldn't be as much fun, Tom. Since we know the place so well, we'd probably tag you right off. This way, it'll be a real challenge for you."

"I'll say," said Tom. He was looking around, trying to memorize the whole yard.

"Plus," said Mama, "we thought that instead of tagging somebody, you get to kiss them."

"What?" asked Tod. "Who gets to kiss who?"

"I guess that remains to be seen," said Mama, "depending on who you catch. But maybe Louise and I can help out on that score, and arrange to make sure you meet up with the right person."

"It's about time!" said Tom. "I've been trying to arrange a kiss with the right person for a long time." He looked at Mama meaningfully.

"Me, too," said Tod. Then he hiccupped.

"Louise, why don't you go wake up Delilah while I blindfold these folks?" said Mama. "I know she'll enjoy this game."

"How ridiculous!" Maybelle huffed, but she stood still while Mama tied the handkerchief around her eyes.

"You never know," Louise called from the porch steps as she went to get Delilah. "You might get what you always wanted, Maybelle."

"Me, too," said Tod.

"It's not likely," said Maybelle, "playing this silly game."

"We'll see," said Mama. "That's the fun of playing blindman's buff our way. I think I can promise that you'll all get something you've always wanted."

By the time Louise led Delilah out into the yard, blinking from her nap, the four Watkinses were blindfolded and lurching around with their hands held out in front of them to feel their way and catch somebody. Tod had already banged into a fence post. Even at the best of times, without being blindfolded or imbibing several glasses of elderberry wine, Tod was a little awkward on his feet. "Yeeeouch!" he yelled, tripping over a stone.

"I tell you what," Mama called. "I think it's about time to give you that little bit of guidance we promised."

"I'll say," grumped Tod.

"Past time," Tom shouted, charging toward Mama's voice.

Mama moved quickly away from the spot where she had been standing. She took Delilah's hand, stood her in the center of the yard, motioned Louise to lead Willie out of the pigpen, and kept moving while she called out hints.

"All right, Tom, a little to the left. Tod, you're way over by the road. Move toward your right and then keep going. Maybelle, you need to take some steps backward and then turn around."

Step by step, Tom and Tod moved closer to Delilah, whose hand Mama still held. Step by step, Maybelle moved closer to Willie, who stood as tall as he could on his four pig hoofs. Luke flailed around in circles with nobody paying any attention to him.

Louise watched the sky. Between the last pink light and the blue night shone the moon, curving thin and white as the end of a fingernail. And sure enough, below it was the evening star, looking like a diamond ring on somebody's finger.

Louise took a deep breath and stepped into the center of the circle, where the lines all crossed. "Star light, star bright, first star I've seen tonight. I wish I may, I wish I might, have the wish I wish tonight. *I wish for those in the circle who belong together to come together in their true forms.*"

At the same moment Tom stumbled up against Delilah and kissed her on the left cheek, and Tod stumbled up and kissed her on the right cheek.

Maybelle fell over Willie, sat up straight, and—still blindfolded—met him mouth to snout.

Luke crashed into Louise and gave her a big smack on the lips.

Mama sang the first words of "Hush, Little Baby" in a clear, beautiful voice.

Molly Cow answered with a long *moo* from the

barn, the owl hooted a long *whoo* from the tree, and the shoats shrilled short squeals beside the slop trough.

For a moment, the whole world blinked like the star above.

CHAPTER 23

A New Balance

A loud crack broke the silence. The branch where the owl had been sitting hurtled to the ground. There, among broken twigs and bright green leaves, lay Jack Tolliver, looking a little bit dazed but otherwise fit. Two feathers nestled in his reddish-brown hair, and he blinked his round, greenish-brown eyes exactly like the owl, which was nowhere in sight.

A squeal pierced the sky, and an enormous pig dashed between the legs of Tod and Tom Watkins, knocking them off their feet. She raced toward the pigpen and stuck her snout joyfully through the fence, where all the little shoats gathered around with more squeals of their own.

A deep sigh came from the other side of the pigpen, where Maybelle had thrown her arms around a handsome lad who looked remarkably like Willie but was considerably thinner. He had traces of mud here and there, but otherwise his body was bare. Fortunately, Maybelle's full skirt covered him, and she had a blindfold on. Her eyes were closed, anyway, because she was kissing him like there was no tomorrow, and he was kissing her right back.

Louise pushed Luke out of the circle and ran to grab Delilah's huge dress, which was dragging from one back hoof. She threw the dress over Willie's bare body just as Maybelle pulled back to untie her blindfold.

Mama ran over to her husband, dropped on the ground, and circled him with a huge hug. She also circled him with her long, fringed shawl, since the leaves and twigs didn't quite cover him up.

Tod and Tom Watkins, looking as dazed as Jack Tolliver, slowly untied the blindfolds from around their eyes.

"What in the world is happening around here?" asked Tom.

"That's what I say," said Tod. "What in the world is happening around here? I thought I was going to kiss Clara and get exactly what I wanted after all these years."

"Me, too," said Tom. "That's what I thought. Finally, after all these years."

"And there's your old sow back, Clara. Where did she come from?" asked Tod.

"Seems like she just appeared out of nowhere," said Tom.

"Not to mention Jack," said Tod.

"With a shawl on," said Tom.

"Seems like he just kind of dropped out of the trees," said Tod.

"Just so," said Tom.

"And here we thought we were finally going to get what we always wanted," said Tod again.

"What we always wanted was Clara, and now we're never going to get her," said Tom. He put his hand on his brother's shoulder. Tod reached over and put his hand on Tom's shoulder.

"Brother Tom."

"Brother Tod."

"Jack," whispered Mama.

"Clara," said Jack.

"Uhnk, uhnk," grunted Delilah.

"Uhnk, uhnk, uhnk," said the shoats.

"Willie," breathed Maybelle.

"Maybelle," sighed Willie.

"Do we get to eat now?" asked Luke.

• • •

The house was shiny clean with bunches of wild-flowers set all around. Mama had made every one of Willie's favorite dishes. His favorite human dishes. Fried okra, fried green tomatoes, fried potatoes, fry bread, and fried pies. She had left out the fried bacon. There was still plenty of elderberry wine, though, not to mention milk-and-honey. They all sat around the table long after the first star had been joined by all the other stars, and the sky glowed with them.

"Do you think stars get lonely?" asked Louise. "They're so far away from each other."

Jack looked at his daughter softly and hooked his thumb on the overalls Mama had brought him to put on under the owl tree. "Who knows about stars," he said. "Maybe they sing light to each other. Or maybe each star stays by its own self. Some people are happy like that."

"Not me," said Maybelle. "I just about died when Willie went away. I can't believe he's back. What were you doing in that dress, anyway, Willie?"

Willie—changed into a clean shirt and pair of pants—turned bright red, to the roots of his white-blond hair, and dropped his sky-blue eyes.

"I just . . . I just wanted to fool you, Maybelle, a little surprise for the party, pretending to be Mama's long-lost relative Delilah."

"You ever try to fool me again like that, Willie Tolliver, and you'll end up fried bacon."

Willie shivered.

Maybelle reached out and took his hand. "But I know you won't," she said quietly.

Maybelle's nicer than I thought, thought Louise, but not as nice as Willie thinks. Oh, well, you can't pick your relatives. And it looks like Maybelle and I are going to be sisters-in-law for sure. She felt a sharp kick under the table and looked up to see Luke laughing at her. "Stop kicking me, Luke Watkins."

"I asked you three times to pass the salt," he said. "Please."

Louise passed the salt. It turned out she may not have needed Luke in the circle after all, but who knows? Maybe . . . well, if he behaved himself, he wasn't so bad to have around. She passed him the pepper, too.

"What I'd like to know is, what happened to that pig that came charging out of the woods right after Willie . . . uh . . . left a while back," said Tod.

"You mean my pig?" asked Tom. "The one that ran away from my pigpen to Clara's place here? The one that was standing right in the pigpen *before* I got blindfolded and wasn't there *afterward*?"

"That pig is a mystery to me," said Mama. "He disappeared just as quick as he appeared in the first place. I guess that takes care of your complaint, Tom."

"You wouldn't be planning to hang a couple extra hams out in your smokehouse during the next day or two, would you now, Clara?" Tom asked suspiciously.

"Certainly not, Tom. You know me to be an honest woman. Ask Sheriff Tod to check anytime. The smokehouse is empty and it's going to stay that way. You won't find a smidgen of bacon, ham, sausage, chops, or any other kind of pork in this house."

Willie shivered again.

"Have you caught a chill, Willie?" asked Maybelle. She hooked her arm in his.

Luke made a little gagging sound. Louise kicked him under the table.

"Well, I guess we won't be having that pig at the Labor Day barbecue, like I hoped," Tom said, sighing.

"I guess not," said Tod. They looked both sad about not having a pig, and happy about having a brother. It was a peculiar expression—down-mouthed but bright-eyed.

"I guess we'll just have to go heavy on the baked beans and Blue-Ribbon Chocolate Cake," said Mama.

"I wouldn't mind a bite of that Blue-Ribbon Chocolate Cake," said Jack. "It's been a long time, and field mice just don't taste the same."

"Oh, Daddy, that's disgusting!" said Louise.

"Well, each creature has its own ways," said Jack.

Tom and Tod stared at them. "What in the world are you two talking about?" asked Tod.

"You wouldn't know, Tod," Mama said coldly. "You didn't even know Jack was still alive."

Tod and Tom stared at each other uneasily.

"Well, now, Clara, that must have been some kind of false report I got," said Tod.

"Must have been," said Mama. But she didn't press him. The less said the better, as far as Jack's suddenly showing up alive and well after all these years.

"I don't suppose," Tom said slowly, "that you'd want to tell us where you've been, Jack, and why?"

"You wouldn't understand if I did," said Jack. "I'm not sure I understand it myself. Let's just say I wanted to fly, and it went awry. You have to be careful what you wish for in this world."

"Amen to that," said Louise.

"But some things you wish for come true," Willie said, gazing at Maybelle.

"Like Blue-Ribbon Chocolate Cake?" Luke asked hopefully.

"That's an easy one," said Mama. She went into the kitchen and struck a match to light twelve candles for Louise's big-magic-bang early-birthday party. As she walked back into the dark room with a dark cake lit up like stars, they sang, "Happy Birthday to you . . ." Luke sang the loudest and a little off-key. Louise took a deep breath to blow the candles out.

"Don't forget to make a wish," said Luke.

Louise looked at Luke and smiled, but she did not make any wishes.

Epilogue

Years of kisses and pigs went by, but Louise never forgot her twelfth birthday party—or what happened afterward. She could still feel what she felt that night, too excited to sleep after the company went home. She had lain in bed a long time looking out the window. The new moon curved like a cow's horn, with the bright star shining happily beside it. The more she tried to stay still and keep her eyes closed, the more wiggly and wide awake she got. Finally, she decided to go out to the barn. Being with Molly Cow always calmed her. She slipped from her bed and through the house without making a sound so as not to wake up the rest of the family. Outside in the pigpen, Delilah and the shoats were *Uhnking* at each other contentedly.

The night was as clear and beautiful as Mama's voice. Right now, maybe she and Molly Cow would hear the stars singing to one another.

The barn was cool and dark and quiet. Louise listened for the sound of Molly Cow chewing her cud, but heard nothing. She felt her way toward the wooden stall. There, by the dim light of the barn window, she could see Molly Cow lying with her legs folded under her as though asleep, or praying, her head bowed down to the ground. "Molly Cow?" said Louise. "Molly?"

Molly Cow did not move. She was not asleep, not even breathing, an old friend gone to rest.

Louise knelt down. "Oh, Molly," she cried.

"Louise," a quiet voice spoke behind her.

Louise turned but could barely see her daddy's face through the tears. "Did Molly die from the spell? I thought I was fixing it so everybody got what they needed." She fell silent and tried to rub her eyes dry.

"Maybe Molly Cow needed to go, Louise. She was old, a lot older than you."

Louise felt her daddy's arm circle her shoulders. Then she looked down at Molly Cow and started to cry again. "It was too much. I shouldn't have mixed up the wishes and kisses and spells and stars and songs and pigs and cow and owl."

"Well . . . but nature and magic are kind of mixed

up, aren't they? A kiss is natural and a kiss is magical, both at the same time."

Louise thought about Luke's kiss. "I didn't know," she said.

"Listen, my aunt Sadie Tolliver knew everything. What she'd forgotten would fill up your whole brain and slop out both your ears. And Sadie always said how nature's magical and magic's natural. It's kind of surprising. Tomorrow is always a surprise—that's what your mama used to say."

"She still does."

"It still is."

"I used to think surprises were nice," said Louise.

"Some of them are."

"Some of them aren't."

"You're right."

"But Mama said you would help me!" yelled Louise. "She said I was like you and you were like magic." Louise felt a dark rage rising.

"I'm human, Louise, thanks to you. And your mama is more magic than she knows. Come on to bed now," said Daddy. He leaned over and gestured with his hands, as if to play a song on Molly's harp horns. Then he straightened up and waved a blessing over her. "We'll bury Molly Cow tomorrow, by the tree where the Tolliver Owl used to sit."

"And Mama can sing her a lullaby?"

"You and Mama both."

She took her daddy's hand, and they walked up the path to the house, with Old Giant stretched peacefully above them, under the moon and stars.